Spinosaur Island

Donald W. Kruse

ZACCHEUS ENTERTAINMENT
Minong, WI

Spinosaur Island by Donald W. Kruse is published by:

ZACCHEUS ENTERTAINMENT

Zaccheus Entertainment
P.O. Box 23
Minong, WI 54859

ISBN: 978-0-9994571-2-2

1st Edition copyright 2008

2nd Edition copyright 2018

Cover Illustration by Craig Howarth

Manufactured in the United States of America

A special thank you from the author to Craig Howarth.

To Lilda,
my favorite editor

ACKNOWLEDGMENTS

I thank God for the gift of writing, and I thank my wife, Marilyn, my kids, Don and Heather, and my grandkids, Blake, Colin, Shane, and Jolan for their undying love and support. Also, a very special thank you to Ms. Phyllis Diller, who taught me, "Onward and Upward!" I love you, my lady.

One million years ago, somewhere in the vast Pacific Ocean, was an island lush with tropical forests, exotic flowers, and colorful birds. A race of primitive but peaceful people lived there in tree huts built high above the forest floor. There, they were safe from the bone-crushing jaws of the night creatures. For this was no ordinary island in the Pacific. This was an island filled with terror—an island steeped in monsters twenty feet tall and weighing more than seven tons. This was an island where every man, woman, and child lived their lives in constant danger. This ...was Spinosaur Island.

Chapter 1

Fourteen-year-old Troy awoke in his straw cot. As he lay on his back, staring at the thatched ceiling of his tree hut, birds chirped and flitted outside his open window. Early morning sunshine flooded his room, and a slight breeze carried the sweet fragrance of honeysuckle to his nostrils. Suddenly the basketball-size head of a Saltasaur—a long-necked, leaf-eating dinosaur—appeared in the window. Although the window was thirty feet above the forest floor, the Saltasaur had no problem reaching it with its long, thick neck. When standing on its enormous hind legs, it could reach even higher into the canopy of treetops where it fed almost nonstop during the day.

Troy jumped out of his cot and scurried to the window. Neatly piled on the plank floor beneath the window was a bunch of fern leaves that Troy had picked earlier in the week and had stored them there. Reaching down, he grabbed a handful of the succulent green leaves and fed them to the Saltasaur. "Here you go, Panga," said Troy, stroking the friendly dinosaur's head as it chewed. "You're up early this morning."

The tame beast blinked its large, doe-like eyes and continued munching quietly.

Troy scratched Panga's chin, as he fed the last of the leaves to the gentle giant. "That's all for today, boy. Off you go."

With that, Panga withdrew his head from the window, and Troy watched the dinosaur lumber away, dragging its humongous tail on the forest floor.

"See you tomorrow," Troy called after him.

"Troy, are you up yet?" a voice yelled from the next room.

"Yeah, Mom, I'm up," Troy answered, slipping into his shorts, vest, and sandals—all handmade from leather.

"Don't forget to stop off at Chief Creta's hut this morning," Troy's mom said.

Troy liked Chief Creta, who was a kind and elderly gentleman. He looks like somebody's grandfather, Troy thought, with his gray hair, twinkling blue eyes, and ever-present smile. He was the Chief Commanding Officer of Spinosaur Island, cheerful to his fellow citizens, and always striving to keep the land a happy, peaceful village. The warmth and kindness that radiated from Chief Creta made Troy feel safe and secure in a way, as though everything in the world was okay when the old gentleman was around. And he loved the Chief's easygoing ways and his mild sense of humor.

"What do I have to fix at Chief Creta's this time?" Troy asked, standing over a wooden washbasin, washing his face.

"He needs you to fix a couple of honey pails that keep leaking," his mom answered from the other room. "He says you're his favorite handyman."

Troy chuckled at that and dried his face with a burlap towel. "I'm *everyone's* favorite handyman."

Troy was well known throughout Spinosaur Island for his ability to fix almost anything. Chief Creta was always asking him to stop by and repair a leaking honey pail, or a broken step, or a cracked table leg. Once it was the thatched door to Chief Creta's hut that had shut too tightly and had stuck in place. Chief Creta was too old and too frail to struggle with it, so Troy had come over and fixed it by rehanging it on new leather hinges.

But mostly it was the old wooden pails that needed constant mending. The pails were used by everyone on the island for storing water or honey inside their huts. If a pail had a hole in it, Troy would promptly patch it with a wooden plug that he carved from a branch. If a pail had a crack in it, he would quickly seal the crack with his own putty-like invention. He made the putty by mixing tree sap and beeswax with clay he had dug up from the ground. The putty always worked quite well. Whether they were wooden honey pails or wooden water pails, once Troy fixed them, they stayed fixed. Before he had invented his putty, all the cracked pails had been thrown away. No one else had known how to fix them. The villagers called his invention pail-putty.

And that made Troy feel proud of himself. Besides getting satisfaction from fixing things, he also enjoyed the praise lavished on him by his fellow islanders every time he fixed something for them. He especially enjoyed the compliments and gratitude given by the adults. Being able to do something that none of the grown-ups could do was a healthy boost to his ego.

"Come and eat your saltberries before they get cold," his mother called from the kitchen.

Troy entered the kitchen, gave his mom a peck on the cheek, then sat down at a wood plank table. His mom placed a bowl of warmed, mashed saltberries in front of him. After pouring honey on them from a wooden pitcher, Troy dug in. In between bites he said, "You know, if I stop off at Chief Creta's, I'll be late at the saltberry field."

The saltberry field was big—as big as a football field. It was surrounded by an enormous wall of twelve-inch-thick oak logs that had been driven vertically into the ground, side by side, and lashed together across the top with leather thongs. The wall stood fifteen feet high—tall enough to keep out the Spinosaurs. At the north end of the field was a colossal gate, also built of oak logs that were lashed and pegged together horizontally. Its thick leather hinges had been made from Spinosaur hide. Next to the gate, just inside the fence, was the storage tree. The storage tree supported a thatched storage shed built high in its branches. There, the islanders stored their hoes, rakes, shovels, wooden pails, leather seed bags, and saltberry seeds.

Saltberries were the only food that the islanders could eat—besides honey. Their primitive bodies simply could not digest anything else. If someone were foolish enough to eat something other than saltberries or honey, he or she would become violently ill ... or perhaps even die.

The honey was collected daily from wild beehives scattered throughout the forest inside hollow trees. But the saltberries had to be planted in the field every day. The white, fuzzy, baseball-size berries grew to full size overnight. By the next morning, they were ready for picking. And after they were harvested, a new crop was immediately planted in their place. Thus, the planting and harvesting of the life-sustaining saltberries was a daily routine that had been going on since anyone on Spinosaur Island could remember. The only problem with saltberries was that they were salty— very salty—and consequently, everyone who ate them had an elevated salt content in their body.

Unfortunately for the islanders, Spinosaurs craved salt. They viciously attacked and devoured anything that tasted salty—including saltberries and the islanders themselves.

"Don't worry," Troy's mom said, removing dirty wooden dishes from the table. "Chief Creta will excuse you from your field work while you're fixing his pails. Doesn't he always?"

Troy washed down his saltberry breakfast with a cup of water, then handed the empty cup to his mom. "Then I'm off," he said, opening the thatched door and starting down the winding stairs that would take him to the forest below.

"Could you bring home more firewood today?" his mom called after him.

Without looking back, he waved his hand and said, "Sure thing. See you later, Ma."

"Goodbye. I love you."

"Love you, too," he said, then headed straight for Chief Creta's hut. Daytime on Spinosaur Island was a relatively safe time. Usually it wasn't until after nightfall that the Spinosaurs began roaming through the forest, hunting for their next meal. Spinosaurs were enormous, flesh-eating dinosaurs forty feet long, twenty feet tall, and weighing seven tons or more. They had huge crocodile-like heads, with powerful jaws studded with razor sharp teeth. Growing out of their backbones were giant sails made up of spike-shaped spines of bone, joined together by a thick layer of leathery skin. They were horrible-looking creatures with ferocious tempers and insatiable appetites. Their keen sense of smell enabled them to easily detect the salty scent emitted by all islanders and the friendly Saltasaurs alike. No wonder man and beast *both* feared the night.

When Troy arrived at Chief Creta's tree hut, he found the old man was his usual jovial self, and Troy felt right at home there. In fact, since Troy had lost his father two years ago from a Spinosaur attack, Troy sort of adopted the elderly Chief Commanding Officer as his father figure. Chief Creta had been kind and helpful to Troy and his mom during their time of need. No one could ever take the place of his real father, of course, whom Troy had loved dearly. But Chief Creta had done an excellent job of filling a certain void in Troy's life after the tragedy. He was grateful for the friendship and the caring the Chief had given them.

After fixing the honey pails, Troy announced cheerfully, "All done. These should last you a very long time."

"Oh, I don't doubt that, my boy," Chief Creta replied smiling. "You do nice work." He placed a wrinkled hand on Troy's shoulder. "Now, did you have any breakfast yet?" His merry blue eyes twinkled beneath gray bushy eyebrows.

"Yes, Sir, I did," Troy answered. "Thank you."

"Oh, thank you, my boy. Thank you." He extended a fragile hand, and Troy shook it warmly.

"Now I'm off to the saltberry field," Troy said. "Take care of yourself."

"Don't be a stranger," said the Chief. "Stop by anytime ... and say 'Hi' to Officer Shuno. If he questions your being late this morning, tell him I've already excused your absence."

"Will do," Troy called over his shoulder, then started down the winding stairs. When he reached the bottom, he turned and headed for the saltberry field where he would work the remainder of his eight-hour shift alongside his fellow islanders, including men, women, and children.

Because there was no such thing as school on Spinosaur Island, the small children stayed at home with their mothers and played all day. The teenaged children, however, were expected to work in the field with their parents. Growing the saltberries was an extremely important job since everyone on Spinosaur Island depended on the unique berries for their very existence. The grueling, daily work routine made children grow up fast on Spinosaur Island. At the saltberry field, Troy entered the gate and was heading for the storage tree hut to get his tools, when he heard someone shouting behind him.

"WHERE HAVE YOU BEEN?"

Troy stopped dead in his tracks and turned around. Glaring at him with flared nostrils, bulging eyes, and hands on his hips was Officer Shuno.

Officer Shuno was the Second Commanding Officer of Spinosaur Island. He was in charge of the saltberry field, supervising the daily planting and harvesting of the saltberry crop. Unlike Chief Creta, Officer Shuno was not the warm and friendly type. Only middle-aged, he was built like a bull and had the temperament to match—at least whenever Chief Creta wasn't around.

"Hello, Officer Shuno," Troy said, forcing a smile. "I was at Chief Creta's hut, fixing his honey pails. He said to tell you that he's already excused me for being late."

Enraged, Officer Shuno marched up to Troy and towered over him, his red bloated face only inches away. "Maybe Chief Creta has excused your tardiness," Officer Shuno spat through clenched teeth. "But *I* haven't."

Troy felt his heartbeat quicken and his stomach tighten. His mouth hung open, speechless.

Officer Shuno ranted on. "Do you know who *I* am? I'm the Second Commanding Officer on this island, and in case you've forgotten, that means I'M YOUR BOSS!"

The people working in the field, standing closest to Troy and Officer Shuno, stopped their work and stared. For a moment, there was dead silence, then the raucous cawing of crows flying overhead shattered the stillness.

Shocked and embarassed, Troy cleared his throat and tried to speak. "I—"

"SHUT UP!" Officer Shuno yelled. "I'm not done talking."

Ever so slowly, Troy felt his embarrassment turn into anger. But he kept still ... at least for now. Is this guy nuts? he thought, biting his lip. Officer Shuno suddenly turned his attention to the curious onlookers and barked, "WHAT ARE *YOU* LOOKING AT? GET BACK TO WORK! ALL OF YOU!"

Like frightened little children, everyone quickly looked away and went back to planting saltberries, their shoulders shrugged, heads hanging low.

Officer Shuno faced Troy again. "Since I didn't give you permission to be late this morning, I find it necessary to punish you."

"What?" Troy asked disbelievingly. "You gotta be kidding!"

Without warning, the back of Officer Shuno's hand caught Troy on the mouth, knocking Troy to the ground. Then he stood over him, straddling him, pointing a thick finger, his face twisted with rage. "Don't sass me, boy. You hear me? Don't you *ever* sass me!"

Sprawled in the dirt, blood trickling from his lip and down his chin, Troy clenched his fists and was about to fight back when Officer Shuno cut in again.

"You will stay here and work in the field until dark. Then, you will clean all the tools of your fellow field workers before you go home tonight."

Troy slowly wiped the blood from his mouth and stared at it on his fingertips. Then he looked up at Officer Shuno. "With all due respect, Sir," he said through clenched teeth. "The Spinosaurs come out at night. How will I get home?"

Officer Shuno reached down, grabbed Troy by his vest, yanked him to his feet, and stood nose to nose. "That's *your* problem," he said, his eyes wild. "But know this ... if you disobey my command, I'll have your *mother* thrown in prison, and *you* will work double-duty in the field for a month!"

At the mere mention of his mother, Troy felt himself bristling with anger. But somehow he knew he was fighting a losing battle with this madman who stood before him, barking in his face. In a matter of moments, Troy's life had been turned upside down, and he didn't doubt for a second that this lunatic would, indeed, have his mother thrown into prison. So in order to spare his mom, he offered no further resistance. He would bide his time and think of a better solution ... later.

"I will do what you command, Sir," Troy said, staring at the ground.

"You bet you will," Officer Shuno snapped. "Now, get to work." And with that, he turned and marched away.

Troy climbed the winding stairs of the storage tree hut, grabbed a wooden hoe and a leather bag filled with seeds, then returned to the field and began his work. First he hoed a trench in the dirt a few inches deep and fifty feet long. Then he dropped little white seeds—about the size of watermelon seeds—into the trench about four inches apart. Then he went back with his hoe and covered the seeds with dirt and tamped the dirt with his foot. All the while, he thought of Officer Shuno's threat, and the thought of his mother being in prison really frightened him. Rumors had it that the prison tree hut on Spinosaur Island was definitely *not* a good place to be.

Some shouting erupted from the other end of the field. Troy looked up and saw Officer Shuno shaking his fist and scolding a group of bewildered villagers laboring under the hot sun.

Shaking his head in disbelief, Troy sighed, then began hoeing another trench. I can't believe he's going to make me stay after dark, he thought. Reaching into his seedbag, he grabbed a handful of saltberry seeds and dropped them, one by one, into the trench. Overhead, he heard the noisy flock of crows and looked up.

"CAW! CAW! CAW!" they shrieked, circling above, apparently eyeing the coveted seeds. Their sleek coal-black plumage shimmered in the sunlight.

"Sorry, fellas," Troy said, covering the seeds with dirt. "You'll have to find your dinner somewhere else." After circling a few times, the crows finally flew away and invaded the upper branches of a cottonwood tree just outside the fence.

Troy resumed working. The sun was still high in the sky. It would be quite a while before he could go home.

When quitting time finally arrived for the other villagers, they trudged from the field toward the storage tree, quietly filing past Troy as he continued his long stretch of punishment. Twice he looked up and saw several of them casting him a sympathetic glance, their faces tired and weary. They piled their hoes and rakes against the trunk of the storage tree hut. None of them spoke.

They don't dare, Troy thought. They're probably petrified. He nodded at them and smiled weakly. I don't blame *them,* he thought, staring at the growing pile of dirty tools being left for *him* to clean. It's not *their* fault. They're only following the lunatic's orders. Frowning, he carefully scanned the field. Where *is* Officer Shuno, anyhow?

Just then, a bluster of screaming and shouting burst at the far end of the field. Troy turned around and saw Officer Shuno badgering a small group of women who brought up the rear of the line. They were cowering from the madman's vocal guns and flailing arms.

Bitterly Troy swung his hoe hard into the ground, gritting his teeth. Lunatic! he thought, and just as he thought the word, someone standing beside him said it out loud.

"Lunatic!"

Troy looked up, surprised. It was his friend Mante, standing alongside Mante's girlfriend, Bree, holding her hand. "That guy's an absolute lunatic!" Mante repeated, staring across the field at Officer Shuno.

"Hi, guys," Troy said, pulling his hoe through the loose dirt. "Better move along before he sees you talking to me."

"How did *he* ever become Second Commanding Officer, anyway?" Bree asked. Her long brown hair curled softly around her pretty face, and her green eyes flashed with anger. More than once, Troy had wished that he had met her first.

"We, the people of Spinosaur Island, elected him," Troy replied in disgust. "Remember?"

"We heard about your punishment," Mante went on, still keeping an eye on Officer Shuno. "We think it's ridiculous. You should report this to Chief Creta."

"How will you get home tonight?" Bree blurted, touching Troy's arm.

Troy noticed the gesture. Looking into her beautiful eyes, he said simply, "I don't know."

"He's coming!" Mante gasped.

Troy turned his gaze toward Officer Shuno who was done berating the women and was now walking toward Troy and his friends. "Get out of here—quick!"

Still holding hands, Mante and Bree fled through the field and out the gate. Soon the last of the field workers were gone, too.

Officer Shuno approached, his hands on his hips, and planted himself in Troy's face. Nodding toward the heap of dirty rakes and hoes, he said, "Don't even *think* of leaving here tonight without cleaning every last one of those tools."

Troy looked at him through squinted eyes, struggling to contain his anger. "Yes, Sir."

Officer Shuno turned to leave, then stopped abruptly. "And don't even *think* of going to Chief Creta about any of this. This matter is between you and me. Understand?"

Troy tightened his grip on the hoe. "Yes, Sir," he said, clenching his teeth.

With that, Officer Shuno turned and marched through the gate, swinging it shut behind him, leaving Troy all alone.

Hours went by and the sun now hung low in the western sky, barely peering over the treetops on the distant horizon. Troy stopped hoeing and planting and walked over to the storage tree. Eyeing the pile of dirty tools leaning against the trunk, he sighed then plunked himself down on the ground and began the tedious job of scraping the wooden tools. Using the sharp edge of a small, flat rock, he scraped and cleaned until darkness settled upon him. He was getting tired and his back ached. Just a few more to go, he thought, and then I can go home. Somewhere in the darkened forest, an owl hooted, then ... silence.

When he was cleaning the last hoe, a loud, piercing squeal shattered the evening stillness.

EEEEEEEEEEEEEE!

Troy jumped up, dropping his scraper but clutching the hoe, his eyes wide with fear, his heart banging in his chest. He stood frozen, straining to hear, waiting for any further noise.

There was none—just the wild beating of his heart.

A light breeze gently rustled moonlit leaves in the surrounding forest.

Then ... silence.

But it was too silent. Troy thought of the lake nestled in the woods nearby. Right now its surface was probably smooth and glassy, reflecting a beam of moonlight that perhaps illuminated a pair of courting loons. On most nights from his tree hut window, he could hear the maniacal laughter of the loons. And the vocal dueling of bullfrogs. And the chirping chorus of crickets. And the incessant whistle of a whippoor-will.

But not on this night. On this night there was only silence.

Another poof of warm air played through the forest. Leaves fluttered and whispered.

And then he heard it again—a screeching squeal in the woods ... in the dark.

EEEEEEEEEEEEEEEEEEEEEE!

The animal-like scream was followed by a blast of grunting and snorting sounds.

All alone in the deserted saltberry field, Troy no longer felt safe. A shiver shot up his spine and his skin crawled, causing the small hairs on the back of his neck to stand erect. The Spinosaurs are getting closer, he thought. I'm outta here!

Frantically, he leaned the hoe he was last cleaning against the fence, next to the gate. Then he ran out the entrance and swung the heavy wooden gate shut. The massive gate closed with a bang, knocking the hoe down. Troy saw it fall into the narrow crack between the gate and the fence. From outside the fence, he pushed on the tip of the handle, trying to force it back through the crack so it would fall safely inside the fence. Gritting his teeth, he pushed and pushed.

A deep, rumbling growl erupted in the darkness close by.

The hoe would not budge. His mind scrambled as a cloud of panic began to sweep over him. Briefly he thought of opening the gate, running back inside the fence, and removing the hoe. But as he reached for the gate, an earsplitting roar almost made him jump out of his sandals.

"Forget this!" He grabbed hold of the long wooden bolt

on the gate and forced it into place. With the gate now safely locked, he turned and bolted through the forest. Racing down the path that would lead him to his tree hut, blood rushed through his veins, and his heart banged with each frantic step.

He was running for his life and he forgot all about the hoe—the hoe that had been held in hundreds of peoples' sweaty hands over the years. The hoe whose wooden handle was saturated with salty perspiration. The hoe that now lay wedged in the crack, with its handle sticking through to the outside of the fence. The hoe that was now exposed and would surely attract Spinosaurs to the saltberry field.

Just when Troy thought he had put a safe distance between himself and the Spinosaurs, he heard a popping and crackling noise in the underbrush behind him.

"Damn!" he cried, feeling a new surge of energy shoot through his body.

The sound of more branches cracking not far behind.

He ran faster, gasping for air, his heart hammering. His sudden spurt of energy was gone now. His legs grew weak and wobbly as he ducked and dodged branches jutting into the pathway. Twice he smacked into them, unable to see them even in the moonlight. His fear was so great, he had barely felt the sting when they slapped his face. Every muscle in his body grew closer and closer to caving in. Mustn't panic, he thought. Got to run faster. Faster. His breathing was fierce. He thought his lungs would burst if he gasped any harder.

The sound of growling close behind. Then silence. Then the sound of dry brush crackling, snapping underfoot.

Troy could actually feel the ground vibrate beneath him— the monster was *that* close. He pressed on. Faster. Faster. Can't stop. I mustn't!

Growling again—thick, deep, and angry.

The noise of cracking brush behind him grew louder, louder, and more frequent. The creature was running incredibly fast, closing in on him.

Suddenly, only a few yards ahead, he could see the winding steps to his tree hut dappled with moonlight. There! he thought. Almost there!

The stairs lay dead ahead, and Troy had never seen anything so welcome, so inviting, so safe in his whole life. Just a few more steps and then ... .

CRASH!

A huge vicious-looking Spinosaur ripped through the brush next to the stairway. Its eyes were slits—red-glowing, mean and hateful-looking slits that locked onto Troy's eyes. It lowered its thorny head, its huge shoulders bulging above, its leathery sail bristling with spines. It growled deep in its throat. Its breath wreaked of something dead and decomposed.

Troy stood frozen with fear, his eyes bulging, his heart exploding.

Briefly the creature sniffed the air, then raised its monstrous head and squealed loud and long.

EEEEEEEEEEEEEEEEEEEEEEEEEEEEEEEEEEEEEEEE!

Then, with nostrils flaring and teeth gnashing, the Spinosaur charged, blocking the path to the stairway.

There was no time to think. No time to panic. No time to run away. Troy knew instinctively that his only chance for survival was to get to those stairs. He raced forward and at the last possible instant, he veered sharply to his left, barely missing the gnashing jaws that popped furiously only inches from his face.

The Spinosaur chased him around the tree with incredible speed for a creature of its size, its growling escalating into hard, vicious snarls. It squealed and grunted hungrily as Troy scurried behind and around the tree trunk, coming up behind the stairway.

Just then, five more Spinosaurs broke through the thick brush and joined the chase, squealing and growling. There was no time to lose, no time to miss. Troy reached up and grabbed the stair railing that was on his right side now, level with his head. Straining every muscle in his body, he swung himself up and over the railing, landing safely on the stairs, just as a half dozen fang-studded jaws snapped shut behind him.

POP! POP! POP! POP! POP! POP!

Terrified, Troy used his last bit of strength to scramble up the winding stairs to his tree hut. At the top, he collapsed on the porch, gasping for air, trying desperately to catch his breath. His heart still pounding, he leaned his forehead against a porch post and peered over the railing at the creatures below. He watched, horrified, as the apparently frustrated monsters pawed and bit savagely at the tree trunk, their long pointed teeth glinting in the moonlight. Their glowing eyes pierced the darkness like red-hot coals straight from hell.

Troy dragged himself inside to the kitchen, where he gulped water from a wooden pail. He drank long and deep, his pulse finally beginning to let up. Staggering to his straw cot, one final thought flashed through his mind before he collapsed: Thank goodness Spinosaurs can't climb trees! Then he rolled onto his side, eyes shut tight, and drifted into a fitful sleep.

Chapter 2

"Troy, where's the firewood you promised me?" his mom called from the kitchen. Frowning, she removed a cold bowlful of cooked saltberries from the table. "And why didn't you eat your supper I left for you yesterday?"

No answer.

"Troy?" Louder this time. Still holding the wooden bowl, she went to his room and poked her head in the thatched doorway. "Troy?"

Troy jerked awake and bolted upright in his straw cot, sweating and panting, his eyes wide with alarm, his heart racing. "Wha—"

"Are you all right?" His mom moved to his bedside and placed her hand on his forehead."You don't look so good ... you feel warm."

"Nightmare," Troy stammered, rubbing his eyes. "Officer Shuno. Spinosaurs. The hoe." Suddenly he tore his hands from his eyes and stared at his mom, shocked.

"What's wrong?"

"The hoe!" Troy blurted. "I forgot about the hoe!"

"What hoe? What are you talking about?"

Still dressed in yesterday's clothes, Troy sprang out of bed just as Panga thrust his blue-green head in the window.

The gentle Saltasaur stared quietly at Troy, obviously waiting for his daily treat.

Troy's mom noticed the absence of fern leaves that were
usually stored on the floor beneath the window. Puzzled,
she said, "You didn't get any firewood and you didn't pick
any leaves for Panga. When did you get home yesterday?"

"Not until after dark," Troy answered, heading for the
door. "Mom, can you do me a favor and feed Panga for me
today? I really have to go now."

"After dark! You could have been killed!"

"I *was* almost killed. I'll tell you all about it later. There's
a fern bush at the bottom of the stairs with big, juicy leaves.
Just give him a handful. Thanks, Mom. Love you."

"But—"

Too late—he was already out the door and flying down
the wooden stairs that spiraled around the tree trunk. Moments later, he was on the path that would lead him to the
saltberry field.

The sun reddened the eastern horizon, and birds roost-
ing in the forest canopy chattered nonstop. Hidden in the
overhead branches, cicadas buzzed loudly, and dew glistened
on fern leaves that lined the dirt path.

Troy felt safe because it was daylight now—although
daylight was not a guarantee that Spinosaurs wouldn't come
out now and terrorize the village. In the past, the ugly beasts
were known to come out occasionally on dark, cloudy days,
or whenever they were too hungry to wait until nightfall for
food. Many of the villagers believed the Spinosaurs were sen-
sitive to sunlight, and they slept during the day in the deep-
est, darkest part of the forest.

The friendly Saltasaurs, however, spent *their* nights in
the ocean that surrounded the island, along the shoreline,
in water deep enough to submerge their bodies and most of

their necks. Like birds, they slept standing up, with only their heads and a small portion of their necks jutting up above the water like tree stumps. There, they were out of reach of the Spinosaurs who never ventured into the ocean.

He walked on, his head lowered and his mind snagged deep in thought. *Gotta get to the saltberry field before anyone else does. Don't want Officer Shuno to see that hoe sticking out of the fence. I didn't even get a chance to clean it. That'll really tick him off. Seems like everything ticks him off lately. Wonder what his problem is.*

He kicked an acorn lying on the path. It skittered a few feet ahead, then stopped. As he approached it, he kicked it again—harder. This time it shot through the air, piercing a wild philodendron plant whose broad, polished green leaves licked the edges of the narrow lane.

"Ouch!" a soft voice cried out from behind the towering plant.

Troy stopped abruptly. "Who's there?" he asked, startled.

The giant leaves began swaying and shaking. "It's only me," the voice called out. Then, after more rustling, the leaves parted and Bree emerged from the brush, carrying a pail of honey. "Hi," she said, smiling radiantly.

"Oh, hi, Bree. Sorry about that. I didn't know you were there."

Dressed in a leather frock, she bent forward and rubbed her bare shin. "That hurt!" But her smile never wavered, and her eyes—those beautiful green eyes—locked onto his. "What was that, anyhow?"

"An acorn. I was kicking an acorn," he said sheepishly. He noticed her wooden pail brimming with honey."Can I carry that for you?"

Still gazing at him, she stood up and handed him the pail. "Thanks. My tree hut is just down the path a little way."

"Yes, I know. "The two of them began walking side by side.Feeling a little awkward, he said, "You're up early this morning."

"Yes, I know," she teased, then chuckled softly. "I promised my folks I'd get us some honey for our breakfast. What about you? You're up early, too. How did you make out at the field yesterday?"

Troy filled her in on the events of last night. When he told her the part about the Spinosaurs almost killing him, she seemed to be very upset.

Without warning, she grabbed his free hand and said, "After we drop this honey off to my parents, I'm going with you to the field. I don't want you to be alone with Officer Shuno. I don't trust him. Ever since he was elected the Second Commanding Officer, he hasn't been the same—not that he was *ever* a nice man."

Troy tried not to let his surprise show—surprised that his best friend's girlfriend would want to hold hands with *him*. Feeling a little guilty, he said nonchalantly, "Oh, I agree. He's definitely *not* the same guy everybody voted for. I think we've all been tricked." He stopped her at the foot of her stairs. Growing on either side of the stairway were honeysuckle bushes dotted with clusters of snowy white flowers. Honey bees buzzed from flower to flower, scooping out the rich, sweet nectar.

He turned and faced her. "Listen, Bree ... I appreciate your concern and everything ... I really do. But I'm a big boy now and I can take care of my—"

"Well, I'm a big *girl*," she interrupted, "and there's safety in numbers. That man is crazy, and I'm going with you. And that's that!" Then, still holding hands, she led him up the winding stairs to her parents' tree hut.

Inside, Bree introduced Troy to her mother and father. Her mother was busy cooking saltberries over an open fire in the cooking pit. The cooking pit was a circular bed of gravel about four inches thick, surrounded by a ring of basketball-size rocks, and situated on the floor in the center of the kitchen. The fire was fueled by short chunks of logs, dried twigs, and shards of bark. In the thatched roof, directly above the fire, was a hole about three inches round which allowed smoke to escape harmlessly. A leather flap, attached to the ceiling next to the vent hole, served as a tiny hinged door that could be closed to keep out rain when the cooking pit was not in use.

"Won't you stay and have breakfast with us?" Bree's mother asked Troy, as she began setting the plank table with wooden bowls, cups, and spoons. "We have plenty."

"Oh, no thank you," Troy replied, edging toward the thatched doorway. "I really have to be going. It was a pleasure meeting you both."

Bree's father looked up from the table. "What's your hurry, son? Have some breakfast."

Bree spoke up and said, "Actually, Dad ... we both have to be going now."

"Oh?" said her mother, pouring water into the wooden cups. "How come?" Troy started to speak, but Bree cut him off."Troy was late in getting to the field yesterday, so he promised Officer Shuno he'd get an early start today to make up the difference." She gave Troy a stern look, signaling him to shut up. "And I promised Troy I'd go with him and help him at the field."

"Well, you'll have to come back another time when you're not so rushed," said Bree's father, spooning honey over his cooked saltberries.

"Perhaps you could join us for dinner some time," Bree's mom said, as she sat down at the table. To her husband she asked, "Can you pass the honey, please?"

Back on the path, heading for the saltberry field, Troy said, "Your parents are nice."

"Yes, they are," Bree agreed. "I'm very lucky."

"They don't work at the field ... do they?"

"No," Bree answered. "My dad works on the construction crew. They build tree huts and stairs. And my mom works with a group of women who make cups and spoons and bowls and pails."

"Oh, I didn't know that," said Troy. "So how come you're not working with your mom, making pails and dishes? That's gotta be easier than working in the field."

"Oh, I don't mind farming. I'm an outdoors girl." She raised her arms, stretching them to either side and said, "Besides, it keeps me in shape—don't you think?"

Troy glanced at her and cleared his throat. "Yes ... very good shape," he said shyly.

Smiling, she dropped her arms and asked, "What about your par—" She cut herself off, and Troy looked at her.

"Sorry," she said.

"It's okay. My dad's been dead for two years now. I can talk about it."

"I didn't mean to bring it up."

"No, no. It's okay. Really," he assured her. "My dad was a really good guy. He was a sandal maker. And my mom is a seamstress. She works with some other ladies, making leather clothes."

"So how come you didn't follow in your father's footsteps and become a sandal maker?"

"I don't mind farming, either. I'm an outdoors guy." Troy raised his arms and made fists, popping his biceps. "It keeps me in pretty good shape, too—don't you think?"

"Oh, I don't know. I hadn't really noticed," she teased, then chuckled.

Continuing along the path, Troy snatched a honeysuckle flower from its bush and began peeling its petals off, one by one. "How come you didn't tell your parents the *real* reason why we're going to the saltberry field so early?" he asked.

"Because then they wouldn't allow me to go with you. They have a tendency to be overprotective. I'm their only child, you know."

"I don't blame them. If you were *my* daughter, I'd be overprotective, too."

She looked at him, smiling. "I'll take that as a compliment."

The path finally spilled into a vast clearing, and just ahead lay the colossal saltberry field. As they approached the massive gate, Troy reached up to unlock the wooden bolt, then stopped suddenly. Something had caught his eye—something behind the thick lilac bushes just to the right of the gate. He moved toward the bushes and his eyes grew wide with alarm. His heart sank and blood rushed through his veins, threatening to burst his temples. Holding his head, trying to take in the enormity of what lay before him, his mind reeled. In the fence, partially hidden by the bushes was a gaping hole—a hole big enough to allow three or four men standing abreast of one another to walk through. On the ground in front of the hole was a hoe with half its handle missing. It appeared to have been chewed off.

Bree grabbed Troy's hand and the two of them stepped through the hole and into the field. Troy's heart sank and his stomach fluttered, as he stared in shocked disbelief.

Bree gasped when her bulging eyes saw it. "How could this happen?"

Lying before them was the saltberry field—a field that should have been overflowing with big, white saltberries—a field that was now dreadfully barren, completely empty, except for hundreds of Spinosaur tracks gouged in the soft soil.

"It's my fault," Troy said, dazed—almost in a trance. "I shouldn't have left that hoe sticking out of the fence last night. The Spinosaurs found it and started gnawing on it. Once they were in a feeding frenzy, they must've kept right on chewing—right through the fence. Then, they went after the berries." He kicked at the loose dirt. "How could I have been so stupid!"

"It's not your fault," Bree said, holding onto his arm. "You shouldn't have been here last night in the first place. Officer Shuno almost got you killed. He caused this—not you. And we have to report this to Chief Creta immediately—before Officer Shuno arrives."

Officer Shuno's threats from the day before flashed through Troy's mind. "He warned me not to go to Chief Creta with any of this. He said he'd throw my mom in prison."

"What! He can't do that! Who does he think he is?" Bree's face grew red with anger. "Now I wish I *had* told my parents what was going on down here. They'd wanta hear about this!"

"You're right!" said Troy, growing angry himself. "He had no cause to punish me. This whole thing could have been avoided." He grabbed Bree's hand."Come on, let's go." He turned and marched back through the hole and out of the field, practically pulling her along.

"Where we going?"

"To the town square. We better alert the entire village *and* Chief Creta."

The time it took to cover the journey to the town square felt like an eternity to Troy. He and Bree had raced through the forest on the dirt path, stopping only once to catch their breath. And although he wanted no harm to come to her and wished that she had stayed home with her parents, he was also glad—very glad—that she was at his side. He was very much aware of the fact that he was growing quite fond of her. But does she feel the same about me? he wondered. And if she does, then what about Mante?

His thoughts were interrupted as they approached a large clearing at the end of the path. By now, sunshine flooded the clearing as the sun slowly continued inching upward. They climbed the four steps to the raised platform that was the town square. The square plank platform was 20 feet by 20 feet, and it was built around the town hall tree.

The town hall tree was a thick, stately tree that grew in the center of the village. In its upper branches was a large, multi-room tree hut. Half of the hut contained the offices of Chief Creta and of Officer Shuno. The other half contained Chief Creta's living quarters.

Hanging from a wooden peg on the trunk of the town hall tree was a white, polished horn that had been fashioned from a Spinosaur bone. It was used by the villagers to alert everyone on the island of any emergency that might occur. Most emergencies on Spinosaur Island were related to the occasional daytime sightings of Spinosaurs. But sometimes the emergency would be a brushfire that had been started by a lightning strike, or an illness that had infected several people at once, or a violent storm that had been spotted out over the ocean and was fast approaching the island. It was a slow and primitive warning system. For after someone blew into the horn, issuing a warning, the villagers would have to assemble at the town square in order to learn what the emergency was. Nonetheless, it was an effective system that had been used by the villagers for eons.

Troy lifted the horn from the peg and held it to his lips. After taking a long, deep breath, he blew into the horn with all his might.

BAA-OOOOOOOOOOU! BAA-OOOOOOOOOOU!

The high-pitched sound sliced through the early morning stillness. He replaced the horn on its peg, then waited.

"While we're waiting," said Bree, "I'll run up and get Chief Creta. He should be the first to know, anyhow. I'm sure he'll want to address the people when they arrive."

"Okay," said Troy, and watched her as she climbed the winding stairs to the Chief's tree hut above. Soon she was out of sight.

Just then Mante arrived, out of breath, his red hair disheveled, his eyes wide with excitement. "Troy, what's wrong?" he blurted, racing up the steps.

"The Spinosaurs have invaded the saltberry field," Troy answered. "They ate the entire crop."

A crowd was beginning to gather now as more and more people arrived. They flocked around the raised platform, pressing against the wooden railings, staring up at Troy and Mante. They looked anxious as they murmured and chattered among themselves, waiting to be addressed by someone.

"Did you forget to close the gate last night?" Mante asked eagerly.

"No, I didn't for—"

"You didn't close the gate!" Mante interrupted.

"Yes, I did close the gate. That's not how they got in."

"Who got in where?" a voice behind them snapped.

Troy turned, and a wave of dread washed over him as he watched Officer Shuno climb the steps, the lunatic's eyes boring into his own.

"I asked you a question," Officer Shuno continued, his scowling face hovering over Troy's.

Mante spoke first."I don't know what this is about, Sir," he blurted. "I just got here. Troy's the one who blew the horn. I was just—"

"Get out of here!" Officer Shuno barked, glaring at Mante.

Troy watched his frightened friend fly down the steps and melt into the crowd that had grown to an alarming size. Everyone in the village must be here by now, Troy thought. But where's Bree and Chief Creta? What's keeping them?

The crowd was growing restless and curious. Their chattering grew louder and louder.

Officer Shuno raised his hands, gesturing for the crowd to be silent. But the crowd kept talking.

"SHUT UP!" he screamed.

Wide-eyed, mouths agape, everyone fell silent immediately.

In the sudden silence, only the twittering of birds could be heard.

Officer Shuno turned his attention to Troy once more. "I'm waiting for your explanation!" he snapped, his voice deep and chilling.

"The Spinosaurs chewed a hole in the fence and invaded the saltberry field last night. There's nothing left to harvest."

"They chewed a hole in the fence! Hah!" Officer Shuno scoffed. He curled his big hands into dangerous-looking fists. They hung at his sides like deadly clubs. He stepped forward, looming over Troy. "That fence has been up for years, and we never had Spinosaurs chewing through it before."

"But, I can show you the damage. It's a huge ho—"

"SHUT UP!" Officer Shuno poked a thick, stubby finger into Troy's chest. "You're a liar!"

It was too much. He had been holding it in long enough. I don't care about his rank or his size, Troy thought, fuming. Enough is enough! "I'm *not* a liar! And don't you ever poke me again, mister!"

Utterly shocked disbelief flashed across Officer Shuno's face. But not for long. Instantly his face reddened and he bared his teeth. "Why you little … ." He grabbed Troy's leather vest with his left hand and raised his right fist, cocking it back, ready to strike. The crowd gasped.

"LET HIM GO!" an old, raspy voice yelled from behind.

Officer Shuno spun around to face Chief Creta who was leaning on a cane and standing next to Bree.

Bree ran up to Troy and threw her arms around him. "Are you all right?"

"Yeah, I'm fine," Troy answered, although his heart was racing and his knees were practically knocking, they trembled so.

Bree leaned close and whispered in his ear. "Sorry I couldn't get here sooner. He's old, you know. It took forever to get him down those stairs."

"It's okay," he said softly, and he was very glad to see her.

"What's going on here?" Chief Creta demanded, frowning at Officer Shuno.

"I'll tell you what's going on," Officer Shuno snapped. "This kid is a liar—that's what's going on!"

Chief Creta raised his cane and pointed it at Officer Shuno. "Since when do we strike our people and call them names? And who authorized you to keep this lad out past dark last night? You damn near got him killed!"

Officer Shuno's face turned purple and his whole body trembled with rage. His eyes were wild, his nostrils flared, hands fisted at his sides. "He says the Spinosaurs chewed through the fence." Officer Shuno raised his hand and pointed at Troy. "And I say *he chopped* a hole in that fence with an axe! It was an act of vandalism due to his rebelliousness!"

"That's not true!" Troy blurted.

"How could you tell such a story!" Bree spat, staring defiantly at Officer Shuno.

"SILENCE!" Chief Creta commanded. Then, to Officer Shuno he said, "Bree has already told me what happened last night and this morning. And I believe her—every word of it." He studied Officer Shuno carefully through squinted eyes. "I don't know what's gotten into you lately, but I want to see you in my office. There are some things I want to discuss with you." He looked at Troy and said, "Since you're the best handyman on the island, I want you to take charge here for the time being." Then he addressed the crowd, filling them in on what had happened at the field. "I'm putting Troy in charge until further notice." Turning to Troy again, he said, "Instruct them to repair that hole in the fence and plant a new crop of saltberries. We can't afford to lose *two* day's worth of crop."

Troy jumped to attention. "Yes, Sir!" He couldn't help but smile—the surge of pride was overwhelming. He faced the crowd, beaming. "All right, everyone," he yelled. "Let's all get down to the saltberry field and get that fence mended. I'll need ten volunteers for cutting new logs. The rest of you can start planting a new crop."

The villagers came alive, chattering loudly as they hustled to the field. Chief Creta winked and smiled at Troy. "Atta boy!" Then he turned and hobbled on his cane toward the stairs to his office above. "Come along, Officer Shuno. We've got some talking to do."

Officer Shuno started to follow the old Chief, then glanced over his shoulder at Troy and grinned evilly. He had the look of a wild animal—mean and dangerous.

The two officers disappeared up the staircase.

Troy couldn't get that evil grin out of his mind, and a cold shiver ran up his spine.

Chapter 3

"All right, everybody! It's quitting time!" Troy shouted, his hands cupped around his mouth. He stood on the porch of the storage tree hut and watched his fellow villagers trudge from the field to the storage tree, their tools slung over their shoulders. They sure worked hard today, he thought, patching the hole in the fence and planting an entire field of saltberries. It was quite a day. And tomorrow there will be berries to pick. Lots of them.

But the best part was, nobody had seemed to mind that Troy was in charge. He had been afraid that some of the older people might resent him for being their boss for a day. But no one had resented him. Everyone had worked in harmony. There had been no complaints, no shouting, no fighting ... and no Officer Shuno.

As he walked stiffly down the storage tree stairs, he became aware of just how hard *he* had worked today, too. His muscles were sore and rigid, and he was exhausted. Having just finished scraping his hoe clean and putting it away in the storage shed, he was glad to be done with that last chore for the day. Time to go home, he thought, as he made his way down the spiral stairs. Wonder how Chief Creta made out with Officer Shuno?

When he reached the bottom, he saw Bree and Mante walking toward him. Something was wrong. Bree had been crying, and Mante looked *very* upset.

"Hi, guys! What's up?" Troy said cheerfully.

Bree forced a smile—her eyes red and swollen—but she didn't answer.

"We have to talk," Mante said—dead serious.

"Oh, I don't like the sound of *that*," Troy said. "What's wrong?"

"Not here," said Mante. "Can you come to my hut? We can talk over a game of flick-sticks."

I have to be going," said Bree, her voice trembling. "I promised my parents I'd come home right away—with everything that's been going on—"

She leaned forward and pecked Troy on the cheek. "See you tomorrow."

She turned to Mante and said, "I'm sorry. I really am." And then, wiping away her tears, she walked through the gate and out of the field.

Stunned, Troy looked at Mante and asked, "What was *that* all about?"

"Can you come to my hut or not?" Mante asked, his voice strained.

"Ah, yeah, sure. But first I have to go home real quick. My mom needs more firewood. And then I'm gonna stop off and see Chief Creta. He'll wanta know how it went here today."

Mante frowned and his face reddened.

"But, yeah, sure," said Troy. "We'll still have plenty of time to play a few games of flick-sticks. I'll see you in a little while."

"Good." Spinning on his heels, Mante kicked a clump of dirt ... then another, and marched out of the field.

A flock of geese flapped their wings high over the field, their spastic honking filling the air. Troy watched as their "V" formation disappeared over distant treetops. A light breeze whispered in his face, drying the sweat on his brow.

When the last of the villagers had gone, he checked all of the tools to make sure that they had been cleaned and properly stored away. There will be no mistakes today, he thought. He glanced one last time at the newly planted field. Then he examined the new log patch in the fence. It was thick, strong, and secure. No way they can get through that, he thought. Satisfied, he stepped through the gate, swung it shut, and locked the bolt behind him. He gave the gate one last tug—just in case—and he was dead certain that it was locked.

On his way home, he gathered dead sticks and branches. He bundled the firewood with a leather thong and delivered it to his mom. After wolfing down his supper of fried saltberries and honey, he went outside and gathered leaves for Panga and placed them neatly on the plank floor beneath his bedroom window. Then, kissing her on the cheek, he said goodbye to his mom and left for the town hall tree hut to see Chief Creta.

Arriving there shortly, he climbed the winding stairs and was met at the door by two guards armed with spears.

"What do you want?" the guard on the left snarled.

Troy was momentarily taken aback. He cleared his throat. "I'm here to see Chief Creta."

"He's busy. Go away!"

"But the Chief will want to see me. My name is Troy and I'm here to report on the field."

"We don't care who you are!" the other guard snapped. He pointed his spear at Troy and thrust it at him, poking him lightly in the stomach. "Now get out of here!"

"Knock it off!" Troy blurted, pushing the spear away.

Just then, the thatched door behind the guards flew open and Officer Shuno jumped outside onto the porch. He stood between the guards, glaring at Troy. "CAN'T YOU UNDERSTAND A SIMPLE ORDER?" he screamed, his face grossly twisted with rage.

Troy was terrified. A sinking feeling in his gut told him that something was dreadfully wrong here. "Y-y-yes, Sir," he stammered. "I-I was just leaving."

"THEN GO!" Officer Shuno shouted, his arm outstretched, pointing his finger.

Troy fled down the winding stairs, going around and around and around—fast as lightning—in spite of his trembling legs. And when he reached the bottom, he didn't stop. He ran as fast as he could, all the way to Mante's tree hut.

* * *

"What do you mean, it's strange?" Mante asked, flicking a six-inch-long willow stick to the far side of the room. The stick sailed through the air, hit the rim of an empty honey pail, then glanced off and fell on the floor. "What's so strange about the Chief being too busy to talk with you?" He flicked another stick. "Maybe he really *is* too busy to talk to you." The stick fell short of the pail. Like the nine sticks before it, it lie strewn on the plank floor around the empty pail. He puffed out his cheeks, then sighed deeply. "After all, he *is* the Chief. Of course he's gonna be busy."

Troy retrieved all ten sticks, then crossed the room and stood next to Mante. Aiming carefully, he flicked a stick. It flew end over end and landed dead center in the pail with a hollow plunking sound. Troy smiled at Mante.

But Mante didn't return the smile. Instead, he gave Troy a disgusted look.

"What about the armed guards?" Troy said. "Since when do we have armed guards at the town hall tree hut?" He flicked another stick that wobbled through the air and into the pail.

PLUNK!

Mante looked more irritated. He folded his arms across his chest and frowned. "Who knows!" he blurted. "We're not officers! We don't know what they do or how they operate! Maybe you're just being paranoid."

Troy was about to flick another stick, but stopped. "What's eating *you?*"

Mante placed his hands on his hips, and his face grew red with anger. "What's eating me? You wanta know what's eating *me?*"

Surprised, Troy's jaw dropped open, and he stared blankly at his friend.

"I'll tell you what's eating me," Mante went on. "You stole my girlfriend—that's what's eating *me!* I thought you were my friend. I thought I could trust you. But the moment my back is turned, what do you do? You steal my girlfriend!"

"Mante, I'm sorry. I really am. But you got this thing all wrong. I didn't steal Bree. She *chose* me. I didn't know it was going to happen. And I didn't try to make it happen. It just ... happened."

"So you admit it—it happened!"

"Huh? Well, no, I mean, I don't know that it *did* happen. I mean, she never said she was *my* girlfriend—did she?"

By now, Mante was fuming. "Don't feed me that stuff! I saw her kiss you at the field today. You've always wanted her—admit it!"

"Mante, every guy our age on Spinosaur Island wants her. Who wouldn't? She's bright. She's funny. She's a hard worker. And she's downright beautiful."

"Oh, that's just great," Mante said, pacing back and forth. "That's just what I needed to hear."

Troy rolled his eyes and bit his lower lip. "I think we better call it a night." He walked over to the pail on the floor and dropped the remaining sticks into it. Then he walked toward the door. He stopped and turned in the thatched doorway of Mante's room. "I didn't plan any of this. And I didn't set out to steal her. I'm sorry. I hope we can still be friends."

"Yeah, right!"

Troy made his way through Mante's tree hut, said goodnight to Mante's parents, then started down the stairs. He heard the door open behind him, and then he heard Mante call out, "I'm still plenty ticked, but from what you've told me about Officer Shuno and his armed guards, I'd stay away from the town hall if I were you. I'll run it past my dad and see what he has to say about it. Meanwhile, you'd better stay away from there."

Then, before he could respond, Troy turned around and saw the thatched door close ... SWOOSH!

Troy continued on his way, heading straight for home.

* * *

The sun faded behind the tree-lined horizon, and darkness crept over the forest once more. In the comfort of his own tree hut, Troy sat on a stool next to the window and listened to the peaceful night sounds: crickets chirping an owl hooting, bats squeaking, tree frogs croaking, and lake loons laughing. A whippoorwill nearby belted out its persistent whistle, and on this particular night, he could even hear the ocean waves in the distant, softly lapping the sandy shore.

Moonlight streamed through his bedroom window and bathed his face. He hadn't bothered to light a candle. Somehow it was more peaceful to sit in the dark while listening to nature's nighttime music. The moonlight set his room aglow in a soft, silvery luster.

Must be beautiful out there right now, he thought. Especially over the lake, with the moon shining so. His thoughts shifted to Chief Creta and Officer Shuno. Maybe Mante is right. Maybe there's nothing wrong at the town hall tree hut. Maybe Chief Creta is too busy to see me. He could be sitting in his office this very moment, writing in his parchment journal, having a meeting, filling out reports, or doing whatever it is Chief Commanding Officers do. Maybe I was just being paranoid about the whole thing. I'll ask Bree what she thinks about it tomorrow. Bree. Beautiful Bree. Troy smiled and sighed deeply. Is she really *my* girlfriend? How did *that* happen, anyway? Not that I'm complaining. Complaining! Hah! I'm the luckiest guy on Spinosaur Island!

Suddenly his thoughts were shattered by the shrill, piercing cry of a Spinosaur somewhere in the distance, in the dark.

EEEEEEEEEEEEEE!

Troy stared at the moonlit forest. How odd, he thought, that something so beautiful, so peaceful could harbor something so dangerous.

There was another piercing cry. Then another.

Then ... silence. Dead silence. Just like that, nature's nighttime music had come to a screeching halt. Now, there was only the distant sound of the ocean waves on the shoreline, and a slight breeze filtering softly through treetops.

A shiver ran up Troy's spine, and his arms and legs tingled with goose bumps.

And then he heard it—a dull, nagging sound far off in the darkness.

What the heck is *that?* he thought. Jumping off his stool,

he leaned over the window sill and stuck his head out into the darkness, straining to listen.

The sound was still there—rasping, scraping—dull and persistent.

A knot formed in his stomach as a feeling of dread engulfed him. It can't be Spinosaurs, he thought, biting his lip. We patched the fence. And I know I locked the gate. And we put all of the tools away. Nothing was left out.

The sound continued—rasping, scraping, gnawing.

He pulled his head inside. It's gotta be a beaver. Down by the lake. They come out at night. Gnaw on trees. Build beaver dams with their logs. Exhausted, he climbed into bed and stared at the window, listening. Yeah, it's gotta be a beaver.

But in spite of his beaver theory, the dull, nagging sound gnawed at his nerves. He tossed and turned into the wee hours of the night. Finally, he slept.

Chapter 4

Troy woke up to the sound of birds chirping outside his window. His room was flushed with bright, warm sunshine. Standing up, he stretched his arms above his head and yawned. Then he noticed Panga's blue-green head already in the window, staring at Troy, waiting for his daily treat.

"Early as usual, I see," said Troy, feeding a handful of fern leaves to the tame Saltasaur. Then he petted its sleek, leathery head. "How you been, boy? Haven't seen much of you lately. Been so busy." He held up another handful of leaves and Panga gently took them with his mouth. "How bout a ride to the field today? Would you like that?"

Panga stared blankly, blinked his big brown eyes, and continued munching quietly. When he finished eating the last of the fern leaves, Troy gave him one last stroke under his chin and said, "Now stay, boy. Don't go away. I'll be down in a little while."

Panga withdrew his head from the room and started grazing the treetop just outside the window.

Yawning again and rubbing his eyes, Troy shuffled across the plank floor to the washstand nestled in a corner of his room. The washstand was a pine frame supporting a pine board countertop. Recessed in the center of the top was a large cypress bowl. He ladled water from a wooden pail and into the empty washbowl. After washing his face and hands, he removed a small piece of leather hanging from a wooden peg on the side of the washstand and dabbed it in the water. Then he began polishing his teeth with the moistened leather. He rubbed them vigorously until he felt with his tongue that they were smooth and clean. Then he put on a pair of clean leather shorts, a clean leather vest, and slipped into his leather sandals. Heading for the kitchen he said, "Hey, Ma! Is breakfast ready?"

His mom burst into the kitchen, her auburn hair a snarled mess. She was jabbing and pulling at it with a wooden hairbrush. "Sorry. I'm running a little late today. Would you mind getting breakfast started? You'll find saltberries in the bottom cupboard, and the honey's on the table." Then she scurried back to her bedroom.

"No problem," said Troy, squatting down in front of the oak cabinets that lined one wall. He grabbed the wooden knob on the cabinet door and gave it a tug. The small wooden door creaked open and he reached inside. He was shocked to see the cupboard so bare, and then he remembered the lack of harvest yesterday due to the Spinosaurs' invasion of the saltberry field. "Our saltberry supply is getting low," he called over his shoulder, while reaching for a berry. "We better get a good harvest today." As he picked up the berry, something hissed inside the cupboard and he saw a flash—a blurring movement—out of the corner of his eye. And at that instant, he felt something strike the berry he was holding, just missing his fingers.

"TROODON!" he screamed, staggering backwards, crashing into the kitchen table and stools. The heavy plank table flipped and went down with a loud crash. The wooden stools toppled over and clattered across the floor.

Troodons were small, flesh-eating dinosaurs, about three feet tall, six feet long, and weighing about 75 pounds. They walked on two powerful hind legs with feet that were armed with deadly claws that could disembowel a man with one vicious kick. Their front legs each sported clawed fingers that could rake off a man's face with one swipe.

Although they were vastly smaller than the Spinosaurs, their claws, teeth, and lightning speed made them a threat to everyone on the island. But most dangerous of all was the fact that the bite of a Troodon was poisonous—like that of a rattlesnake. And just like rattlesnakes, Troodons hissed before they struck.

Terrorized, Troy scrambled to get out of the creature's deadly striking range. He tripped over a stool, lost his balance, fell into a pine shelf on the wall, then thudded to the floor. The shelf flipped off its wooden wall brackets sending candles, cups, bowls, and wooden plates airborne. Then everything came down hard, smashing and splintering on the floor.

The Troodon locked its gaze onto Troy's, stepped out of the cupboard, and slowly advanced toward him, hissing through its pointed teeth with each menacing step.

His heart pounding, Troy sprang to his feet and flattened himself against a far wall. Then he heard his mother hollering from her bedroom.

"Troy, what's going on in there?"

Then he heard the sound of her sandaled feet shuffling toward the kitchen.

"Ma, stay back! Don't come in her—"

But it was too late. Frowning, she entered the kitchen while fastening a button on her leather frock. "What's all the fuss abou—" Then she saw the creature and she froze, her eyes rolling white, bulging with utter panic.

The Troodon swung its small but fearsome head toward Troy's mom. Eyeing her, it flicked its tail and hissed through bared teeth.

"Don't move!" Troy cried. Then, with the predator looking away from him, Troy bent over and snatched the splintered pine shelf from the floor and charged the beast, swinging his makeshift club with every fiber of his being.

The force of the blow sailed the Troodon across the room and into the thatched wall. Troy was on it instantly, clubbing it again and again with all his strength.

Wounded, the creature emitted a horrible scream, scrambled to its feet and leaped out the window and onto a tree branch. Dazed, it clung there for a moment, then lost its grip and plunged to the forest floor.

Troy jammed his head through the window and saw the creature writhing on the ground. Then he noticed Panga who was only a few feet away, his head high in the treetop, munching away. "Panga! Here, boy! Panga, quick!"

Panga lowered his head from the upper branches and was face to face with Troy, staring blankly as he casually chewed a mouthful of leaves.

"Down there, boy!" Troy cried, pointing below. "Get him! Quick!"

Suddenly the Troodon snarled and snapped its jaws as it tried to stand.

Then Panga became aware of the predator lying at his feet. Instinctively, in full defensive mode, Panga raised his massive right front foot above the Troodon, let it dangle momentarily in midair, then slowly brought it down on top of the beast, squashing it to death with eight tons of agitated Saltasaur.

Troy flew down the stairs, two and three at a time. When he reached the bottom, he observed the carnage before him. The mashed carcass was black with green stripes—like all

Troodons—and it was surrounded by a pool of blood. "Thank you, Panga," Troy said, patting the Saltasaur's tree trunk leg. "Way to go."

Panga lowered his slender head, sniffed the carcass, snorted, then returned to grazing in the treetops.

Troy's mom came down the winding stairs, clutching her throat. She stopped on the bottom step, not daring to come any closer. "Is it dead?"

"Oh, yeah," said Troy. "It's dead all right. Panga saw to that."

His mom walked over and stood next to Troy, staring down at the pulverized dinosaur. "How in the world did that thing get all the way up into our tree hut and inside our cupboard?" she asked, folding her arms across her chest.

"Good question," said Troy. "We know for a fact that Troodons are not tree climbers."

His mom looked at him, worried. "Do you think it climbed up our stairs?"

"I guess it's possible." Troy frowned and pursed his lips. "But that doesn't explain how he was able to open and close a cupboard door."

"Then how?"

"Not how, Ma. But who?"

"What do you mean?"

Troy explained to her all of the events that had taken place over the last couple of days, starting with Officer Shuno's hostile behaviour and his threats against Troy and his mom, the hoe sticking out of the fence, the invasion of the saltberry field, the fence repair, and the armed guards at the town hall tree hut.

"And now this," said Troy.

His mom was unnerved."So you think Officer Shuno and his henchmen planted that *thing* in our hut?"

"It's beginning to look that way," said Troy. "I don't see how else it could've gotten in there."

"Then we have to tell Chief Creta about this." His mom ran a hand through her hair and stepped away from the dead Troodon, being careful not to step in its blood. "This situation is getting out of control."

"Don't worry, Ma. I'll figure out a way to get past those guards."

She shot him a look of alarm. "You be careful—you hear me?"

"I will."

"I mean it, Troy. I don't want to lose a husband *and* a son."

"Don't worry," said Troy. "I'll be careful. I promise. I don't want anything to happen to me, either."

"Well, there's no way I can go to work today. My nerves are shot. I'm staying home and cleaning up that mess in the kitchen." His mom pecked his cheek. "You remember to be careful." Then she turned and headed up the stairs. When she was out of sight, Troy heard Mante calling his name.

"Troy! Come quick! They've done it again!"

Troy spun around and saw Mante on the path, running toward him. "What's up?" Troy called, but he had a sneaking suspicion that he already knew.

Mante rushed up to Troy, out of breath, his face flushed and sweaty. "I got bad news. The Spinosaurs have chewed through our new patch in the fence." He gulped air and wiped his forehead with the back of his hand. "They ate all the saltberries again!" Then he glanced at the dead Troodon. "What's this?"

"Damn! I knew it!" Troy stuck his hands on his hips. "That *was* them that I heard last night."

"Heard what?"

"The Spinosaurs," said Troy. "I could hear them gnawing on the fence. I was hoping it was beavers."

"But why would they chew another hole?" Mante asked, puzzled. "There were no tools left out—like last time." He poked the mangled Troodon with his foot. "What happened here?"

"Panga killed it," said Troy. "I'll tell you all about it later." Troy's mind raced with thoughts of Officer Shuno's scowling face once he found out about the new hole in the fence. "Does Chief Creta know about this?"

"Yeah, the guy who discovered the hole went straight to the town hall to tell him. And I came right here to tell you."

"Hopefully he'll be able to get past the guards," said Troy.

"Huh? Oh, yeah. The guards. I forgot about them. Well, I'm sure they'll let the guy through for something *this* important." Mante took another deep breath and wiped away more sweat."So how come they chewed a new hole?"

"Instinct," said Troy.

"What do you mean?"

"Evidently those creatures are going to keep coming back now, chewing a hole in the same spot night after night. It's their instinct. They found food by chewing a hole in the fence in that one spot. So now they know that they'll find it there again and again."

"So what'll we do to stop them?" asked Mante.

Troy's face puckered as he thought hard. "I don't know yet," he said, frustrated. "But I'll think of something. Right now we'd better get back to the field. We can examine the damage and then we'll wait for Chief Creta to get there. Maybe *he'll* know what to do."

Troy looked straight up and called, "See you later, Panga. I have to go now. We'll do the ride another time." Then, to Mante he said simply, "Let's go."

On their way to the saltberry field, Troy told Mante about the Troodon.

"Well, now that you mention it," said Mante, "I remember Officer Shuno walking a pair of Troodons on leather leashes a long time ago."

"What?"

"Yeah, I did," said Mante matter-of-factly. "For real."

"When was this?"

Mante scrunched up his face. "Oh, about two or three years ago. I was swimming at the lake one morning, and I saw him walking along the shoreline with these two Troodons on leashes. He was just walking along and talking to them. I snuck out of the water and hid in that cave right by the shore—you know the one. And I just stayed there and watched him until he left."

"What's he doing with a pair of poisonous Troodons!" Troy cried. "Is he nuts?"

"It is weird, I'll give you that," said Mante. "He must've found them when they were babies and then he raised them and trained them."

"Oh, he trained them all right," said Troy, growing angry. "That's the second time he almost got me killed. And this time my mom could've been killed, too." He kicked a low-lying branch that was overhanging the path. "He's a madman, and I'm not taking it anymore."

When they arrived at the saltberry field, Troy scanned the crowd of excited villagers, searching for Chief Creta. He pushed his way through groups of people huddled together chattering hysterically. Glancing at the faces of every gray-haired man he could find, not one of them was Chief Creta.

"He's probably not here yet," said Mante. "He's pretty slow with that cane, you know."

"Yeah, I know," said Troy, his eyes still searching the

crowd. Suddenly he saw Bree standing with her parents and some other people in front of the new gaping hole in the fence. "There's Bree!" He shoved his way through the crowd, slowly making his way toward her. As he approached, he overheard one of the men talking to Bree and her parents.

"None of this would have happened if that damn kid hadn't left his hoe sticking out of the fence."

"Hi, Bree," Troy said, and then, to her parents, "Hi, nice to see you both again."

The man who had made the ridiculing remark snorted, turned his back on Troy, and walked away. Bree's parents and the others followed, without acknowledging Troy—not even looking at him. "Come along, Bree," said her mom.

Bree crossed her arms, defiant. "I have to talk to Troy."

"Well, don't be long," said her mom, walking away. Then she melted with the others into the crowd.

Bree looked at Troy apologetically. "Sorry about that. They're a little upset because there are no berries to pick again."

"Can you blame them?" Mante blurted. "This is the second day in a row without a harvest. How long do you think our food supply will last?" Before Troy could utter a word, Bree turned on Mante."There's no need to panic. I'm sure we all have at least a few days' worth of berries stored up."

"Yeah, sure," said Mante. "A few days—minus two!"

Troy got that sinking feeling again in the pit of his stomach. "They're all blaming me, aren't they, Bree?"

"Why shouldn't they?" Mante snapped.

"It's not your fault, Troy!" Bree cried. Then, she turned to Mante and said, "You know as well as I do that Officer Shuno caused all of this in the first place. He had no business punishing Troy just because Troy was following Chief Creta's orders to go to his hut and make some repairs."

"Well, if Troy didn't do anything wrong in the first place," said Mante, "then why would Officer Shuno punish him?"

"Because he's jealous of Troy!" Bree yelled. Her eyes became slits and her face puckered. "And so are you!"

"Yeah, right," said Mante. "That'd be the day." His face tightened. "I think you have that backwards." He pointed his finger at Troy. "He's always been jealous of *me*. That's why he stole my girlfriend!"

Troy was taken aback."Now wait a min—"

"I was never your girlfriend, Mante," Bree said, cutting Troy off. "It was all in your own head. I was only your friend. And right about now, we could use a good friend."

"Yeah, well, why don't you go find yourself one?" Mante said, then stormed off, losing himself in the crowd.

Troy was dumbfounded, his mouth agape. Before he could say a word, Bree grabbed his hand and said, "Come on. Let's see if Chief Creta has arrived yet. We'll be able to see better from the storage tree hut."

As they made their way through the murmuring crowd, Troy told Bree all about the Troodon attack at his hut this morning.

"That proves Officer Shuno is out to get you," said Bree, running her fingers through her hair, pulling it away from her eyes. "The sooner we find Chief Creta and tell him, the better."

"Wait a minute," said Troy, spotting a large rock in the field, just up ahead. "I've got a better idea." He climbed up on the rock which elevated him about two feet off the ground. Then he cupped his hands around his mouth and yelled. "Has anyone seen Chief Creta?"

A voice from the crowd called out, "Someone went to get him a long time ago, but he hasn't arrived yet."

Then a different voice—harsh and brutal—roared behind Troy.

"CHIEF CRETA ISN'T COMING!"

The sound of it nearly knocked Troy off his feet. He recognized the murderous voice immediately. It was Officer Shuno's. He gaped in horror as the madman barged his way through the chattering crowd, followed by the field worker who had been sent to get Chief Creta. He, in turn, was followed by two guards armed with spears. And to further unnerve Troy was the fact that these two guards were not the same two he had seen yesterday at the town hall tree hut. How many are there? he wondered. And why?

"GET DOWN FROM THERE!" Officer Shuno bellowed, his glaring eyes like pinwheels.

Troy jumped down and Bree grabbed his hand and leaned into him. "Be careful," she whispered, obviously shaken.

The crowd was immediately silent.

Officer Shuno marched up to Troy, his menacing eyes never wavering. He stood, towering over Troy, his big hands fisted at his sides. He pointed a finger toward the monstrous hole in the fence. "Now look what you've done!" he barked through bared teeth. "This is all your fault!"

Troy felt uncomfortable as the crowd stared at him, their eyes boring into his. But he knew he had to stick up for himself, no matter what. Can't just stand here and let this lunatic convince everyone that it's my fault, he thought. He cleared his throat and was about to speak up when Officer Shuno suddenly stepped up onto the rock and addressed the crowd.

"Chief Creta is not feeling well today," he began.

"Yeah, sure," Troy whispered to Bree, and she nodded in agreement.

"He has asked me to come and investigate this problem. And having inspected this new hole, it is easy to see that we have no choice but to build an entire new fence around this one." He motioned with his hand, pointing to the fence behind him.

Troy jumped with shock. He couldn't believe what he was hearing now. He started to say something out loud to Officer Shuno, but Bree pulled him back. "Shhh!" she whispered, putting a finger to her lips.

"But he's insane!" Troy whispered in her ear. "The Spinosaurs will just chew through *both* fences. Building another fence around the existing fence isn't going to solve anything. He's nuts!"

The crowd suddenly came alive, too, grumbling and shaking their heads. Their faces expressed worry, anger, and disgust.

"They're upset," Troy whispered. "Maybe one of them will speak up and put that nutcase in his place!"

"Shhh!" Bree whispered again.

But no one did speak up. Officer Shuno raised his hands, gesturing silence to the crowd. Then he began, "We mustn't waste any time. The construction of the new fence must begin at once. The sooner you build it, the sooner you can plant a new crop of saltberries."

"What's he talking about?" Troy blurted into Bree's ear, under his breath. "It'll take days to build another fence! Maybe weeks! We'll all starve to death by then!"

"We've got to find a way to see Chief Creta," she whispered back. "This guy has to be stopped!"

"I know you all want to eat," Officer Shuno went on. "So I'm sure you'll all cooperate in building the new fence as quickly as possible. And because you'll all be cooperating in this matter, I trust I won't have to leave my guards behind to watch you. Therefore, I won't." He jumped off the rock and suddenly faced Troy again, glaring at him. "And I trust I won't be getting any more trouble from you," he sneered, his eyes cold and dark.

For an instant, Troy thought about slamming his fist into the lunatic's face. Oh, how he would love to knock the stuffing out of this abusive, demented creep. If only he was big enough. Then he thought of the two armed guards standing on either side of Officer Shuno and realized that a physical confrontation was hopeless. Without the support of the villagers, there would have to be another way to deal with this maniac. So he held his tongue and feigned compliance. "No, Sir," Troy answered solemnly. "I won't be any trouble."

"No, I didn't think so," the Second Commanding Officer snapped. Then he turned and faced the crowd one more time. "Let's get started on this fence, then. You all know what to do. You don't need anyone's supervision. You've built fences before, so get to work. I'll be back tomorrow to check on your progress. I hope for your sakes I won't be disappointed."

Troy watched with contempt as Officer Shuno and his guards busted through the crowd. The villagers tripped over one another, trying to get out of their way. Finally, the lunatic and his henchmen marched out of the field and onto the dirt path. Moments later, they disappeared into the surrounding forest.

Chapter 5

Troy stood with Bree next to the colossal gate, watching the excited, gibbering villagers file past them, most of them not even looking at him. Frustrated, he shook his head in disbelief as they climbed the steps to the storage tree and removed their tools from the shed.

"Look at them, Bree," he said in a low voice. "They're all fools—every one of them. Not one of them has the guts to stand up to Officer Shuno."

"I don't think it's a matter of them not having any guts," said Bree. "I think they blame you for all of this mess, and they really do believe that Officer Shuno knows what he's doing."

"Well, somehow I've got to get them to listen to *me*," said Troy. "I don't understand why they can't see that Officer Shuno is nuts, and his idea to build an entire new fence is insane. It'll never work!"

Bree brushed her hair back out of her eyes. "You and I know that, but obviously these poor people trust Officer Shuno, just because he's the Second Commanding Officer."

"But I have a better idea!"

Just then Troy saw Mante standing in line with the others, waiting to get his tools. Troy waved his hand frantically. "Mante! Over here!"

Mante fell out of line and walked up to Troy and Bree. "What's up?" he asked cooly. "Haven't found a friend, yet?"

The line of villagers continued to file past them, some of them staring curiously.

Troy ignored that last bit of sarcasm. He understood Mante's pain at having lost whom Mante believed to have been his girlfriend. Troy knew he'd feel the same way if he ever lost Bree. But he wasn't losing Bree, and for that he was infinitely grateful. And now wasn't the time to get into it again with Mante. Right now there were more important matters to discuss. Matters of life and death. He needed to get Mante's attention, and get it now. "You're all being stupid—that's what's up."

"Oh, so now I'm jealous *and stupid*," Mante answered, balling his hands into fists, shoving his chest into Troy's.

Bree sprang into action and immediately separated them. "Will you two knock it off already!" she scolded. Then she turned on Troy. "Is that your idea of people skills? You really think you're going to get anybody to listen to you with *that* approach?"

Troy's blood was furiously surging through his veins, pounding in his ears, but he bit his tongue and remained silent.

Then Bree turned on Mante."Do you think you could be quiet for just a moment and give us one minute of your time? Troy has something very important to tell you, and I think you'd better listen." She stepped back and folded her arms across her chest, her eyes flashing.

"Well, make it fast," Mante snapped. "I haven't got all day to stand around and chitchat. We're supposed to be building a new fence—thanks to Troy who started this whole mess in the—"

"Enough!" Bree interrupted. Then to Troy she said, "Tell us *your* idea."

Troy placed his hands on his hips and cleared his throat. "First of all, know this—there's no way building a new fence around the existing fence is going to work. The Spinosaurs will chew through both fences the first night. Secondly, even if we did build another fence, it would take at least a week or more to build it. We'd all starve to death by then. Now, I don't know about you guys, but me and my mom are down to about a two-day supply of saltberries."

"That's about all we have left, too," said Bree.

Frowning, his mouth turned down, Mante said, "Come to think of it, we'll be out of saltberries in about three days."

"Right!" Troy blurted, starting to feel like he was getting somewhere. "So we're all in agreement that we have to start planting saltberries as soon as we can. And we have to make darn sure that the Spinosaurs won't be able to get to them."

"What'd you have in mind?" Mante asked, grudingly.

"Simple!" said Troy. "Instead of building a whole new fence, we just find a boulder along the beach and roll it into place, plugging the hole in the fence. I don't think Spinosaurs can chew their way through rock no matter *how* hungry they are."

"Excellent idea!" Bree cried, making an "okay" sign with her thumb and index finger.

"What's to keep them from chewing a new spot some-where else in the fence?" Mante asked, still frowning.

"I don't know," Troy replied. "They may or may not try to enter at a new spot. But so far, they've only chewed through that one spot. It must be their natural instinct to keep com-ing back to the same spot, over and over, as long as they can chew their way in. But I'm betting they'll scratch at the rock all night for a few nights, and then they'll give up and forget all about our saltberries. It would only take us about half a day to get a boulder into place. And meanwhile, everyone else could start planting a new crop immediately. No need to wait to build another fence before planting a new crop."

"It's certainly worth a try!" cried Bree. "And if the boulder theory doesn't work, *then* we can start building a new fence. What do you think, Mante?"

"Wellll," Mante reasoned, rubbing his chin, "it would be a lot less work."

"You bet it would!" said Troy. "And if it works, then we'll have a new crop of saltberries to harvest tomorrow."

"And then *nobody* has to worry about starving to death," Bree added. "The only thing is," said Mante, "I think we should get Officer Shuno's permission first."

"Are you nuts?" Troy shouted, clenching his fists. "There's no way he's gonna okay *my* idea. You saw how he acted today. He's only interested in his own ideas. He wants to play boss with us. He doesn't really care about any of us. He'd rather see us starve to death before he'd give permission to use *my* idea."

"Then I'm not going along with it," Mante said flatly. "Count me out. I'm not going against Officer Shuno's orders. And neither will you if you know what's good for you."

"Then let's get Chief Creta's permission," Troy suggested. "He's always liked my ideas. I'm sure he'll like my plan."

"Yeah," said Bree. "Let's do that. I've been wanting to talk to Chief Creta anyhow. Let's go see him."

"All right," said Mante."Then go and ask him. You guys don't need me."

"I think it would be better if you went with us, Mante," said Bree."We might bump into Officer Shuno again, and we already know how he feels about Troy. It'd be better if you did the talking—especially if his guards are still around."

"Well, I'm not going," Mante said. "It's Troy's idea, so let him go."

"Yeah, come on, Bree," Troy said, disgusted. "We don't need him."

"If you're afraid to go, Mante," said Bree, "then why don't you just say so? We'll understand."

Mante reddened with anger. "Fine. Let's go then. We'll see who's afraid." He turned and marched out of the field.

Surprised, Troy looked at Bree and smiled. Smiling back, she grabbed his hand and the two of them scampered along, following Mante on the path. On their way to the town hall tree, Troy was glad to be in the lush forest that surrounded them. High above, a green leafy canopy held hundreds of colorful songbirds that chirped and warbled incessantly, flitting from branch to branch. The dirt path lay in a cool, green corridor, bordered on both sides by a mixture of ferns, philodendrons, and castor-oil plants. Spongy moss flourished on tree trunks, rocks, and the path itself. Here was cool relief from the blazing, hot sun.

As the three of them continued on their journey to see Chief Creta, they approached the well by the town hall.

The well was a common meeting place for the villagers, who went there to fetch water. They'd stand around and gossip about the grueling field work, or who had the latest baby, or what the newest saltberry recipes were. The chattering would go on and on.

But now the well was vacant. Most of the villagers were working in the field, but some of the others—like the tradespeople and mothers with young children—were at home, working. Since children were expected to work at a trade or in the field by the time they were only twelve years old, the only schooling they received was the little bit of reading, writing, and arithmetic their mothers taught them before they turned twelve. Then, it was time to learn the life-sustaining art of growing saltberries.

The writing was done on scrolls with porcupine quills dipped in ink. The scrolls were made from Spinosaur hides that had been skinned ultra thin, then stretched on wood frames and left to dry in the sun. The ink was made from the juice of boiled saltberries.

Mante complained of being thirsty, so they stopped at the well to get a drink of water.

He's scared, Troy thought, eyeing his friend suspiciously. He's probably deliberately wasting time, now that we're so close to the town hall—and Officer Shuno.

Mante lowered a pail, tied to a rope, into the blackness. There was a splattering noise as the wooden bucket hit the surface of the water below.

Then Mante began hoisting up the full pail, hand-over-hand.

"How come you're sweating, Mante?" Bree asked. "We're in the shade. It isn't that hot."

Mante didn't answer. He didn't have to.

It's fear sweat, Troy thought. He doesn't want to bump into Officer Shuno anymore than I do.

Mante dipped a long wooden ladle into the pail and drank eagerly. When he finished drinking, the three of them walked over to the town square. Troy led the way up the steps and strolled across the plank deck. He stopped at the foot of the town hall stairs and said, "This is where I let you lead the rest of the way, Mante."

"Uh ... yeah ... sure," Mante said nervously. "No problem. Just follow me, you guys."

"Be sure you insist on speaking to Chief Creta," Bree warned. "I don't think we should leave here until we do."

Mante frowned. "Why do we have to speak to the Chief? I mean, if he's not feeling well, we really don't want to disturb the old guy, do we?"

"I want to see if he really is sick," Troy said. "I think Officer Shuno may be lying."

"Wouldn't surprise me," said Bree.

Mante rolled his eyes, shaking his head. "Let's get this over with."

They climbed the winding stairs, Mante in the lead, then Bree, then Troy.

Two armed guards stood in front of the door to the town hall tree hut, their spears pressed tightly against their sides. Both were husky, but one was taller than the other.

"Halt! Who goes there?" the tall one demanded, as the three of them climbed the last steps and stood on the town hall porch.

Having traded places with Bree, Troy now stood directly behind Mante. He fought to control his trembling, hoping Bree, who was standing right behind him, wouldn't notice.

Mante cleared his throat. As he began to speak to the guards, Troy noticed that he was trembling, too.

"Hello, my name is Mante, and I've come to talk to Chief Creta."

"Chief Creta is sick today. Go away!" the guard barked.

"I'm sorry to hear that," Mante said, his voice quivering, "but I must see him anyway. It's very urgent."

The two guards looked at each other, grinning. Then the tall one stepped forward, looming over Mante. "Perhaps you did not hear me the first time. I said, go away!"

Mante's voice quivered when he spoke. "Uh, we can't leave here until we talk to Chief Creta." He cleared his throat. "It's very important."

The taller guard became enraged. "What's the matter with you? You got a hearing problem?" he snapped. "Now, I told you to get out of here." He placed his beefy hand on Mante's chest and pushed.

Mante stumbled back into Troy. With sheer panic on his face, he turned to Troy and said, "Let's go. We'll come back another time."

"We're not leaving here until we see the Chief!" Troy blurted. Without waiting for a reply, he quickly shoved his way between the two guards and banged on the town hall door. "Chief Creta!" he shouted. "It's me, Troy. Please open up. I must talk to y—"

The guards snatched him up under his arms and held him tightly. He winced as their fingers dug into his flesh. He looked up into their scowling faces. "You seem to be having trouble leaving on your own," the taller one sneered. "Perhaps we can offer you some assistance." He looked at his shorter companion and smiled wickedly.

Still clutching him under his arms, the guards lifted troy off the porch. Then they lifted him higher, inching closer to the porch railing.

Bree screamed, "Stop it! Put him down!"

"You can't do this!" Mante yelled.

Laughing, the guards dangled Troy out beyond the porch. "This is the shortcut," the taller one laughed fiendishly.

Troy gaped in horror at the forest floor below. Mante and Bree begged the guards to stop.

The town hall door opened and Officer Shuno shouted, "Put him down this instant!"

The guards obeyed, and Bree rushed to him and hugged him.

Troy stood in shocked silence. The close call reminded him of the time his neighbors, Mr. and Mrs. Droma, had asked him to build new railings for their stairs, after their little boy had fallen through the old one. The boy hadn't been high up, but it was enough to fracture his leg in two places. It had taken the village doctor, Dr. Hadro, an entire afternoon to set the leg. Troy could only guess what his own body would look like if he had been pitched from the town hall porch. He shuddered at the thought.

"What's going on here?" Officer Shuno demanded.

"These three want to talk to Chief Creta, Sir," the taller guard replied. "I told them he was sick, and I asked them to leave, but they refused." He nodded toward Troy and said, "We were just showing this one here a shortcut home."

The guards threw their heads back in laughter.

"Silence!" Officer Shuno shouted.

He shot a glance at Troy and his two companions. Then his eyes focused on Troy only. "So! It's you again! My favorite little troublemaker. I thought you had learned your lesson the last time you had disobeyed me. But I can see now that I was wrong. Once a troublemaker, always a troublemaker, heh?"

"No, Sir," Troy said, his arms crossed over his chest, massaging his sore armpits. "I'm not trying to be a troublemaker. We just want to talk to Chief Creta."

"He's sick today. Nobody can see him," Officer Shuno said, his hands on his hips. "You got a problem understanding that?"

"No, but I—"

"Then go back to the field and do your work—all of you!"

"Fine! No problem, Officer Shuno!" Bree said curtly. "Come on, guys. Let's just go back to the field and tell the others something terrible has happened to poor old Chief Creta. Maybe we can get a couple hundred people to return with us, to find out what's really going on here."

Bree started for the stairs, but Officer Shuno stopped her.

"Wait!" he said, obviously disturbed by Bree's threat. "What did you want to see Chief Creta about?"

"Well, Sir," Troy said, "there are many of us at the field who don't believe that building an entire new fence is the correct solution to our problem."

He felt ashamed and scared for having lied, but he thought it might convince Officer Shuno to allow them to talk to Chief Creta.

Apparently Bree's threat and Troy's lie worked.

"And just what does everyone believe to be the correct solution?" Officer Shuno asked.

Troy cleared his throat. "Well, Sir, they think it would be easier and more effective to simply roll a boulder in front of the hole in the fence. It would only take about half a day, and we could—"

"Spare me the details," Officer Shuno interrupted, with a wave of his hand. His face was dark and tense, his voice short, impatient. "I'll let you speak directly to Chief Creta. His decision, as always, will be final. Just a moment, I'll get him for you."

"If he's sick," Bree blurted, "maybe we should go in and see him. No sense in making him get up and go outside."

Officer Shuno shot a glance at her. "No! You stay here," he said through clenched teeth. "I'll go get him." He glanced at his two guards, motioning them to keep still.

"But, Sir," the taller one protested, "I thought you said you didn't want anybody to—"

"I *know* what I said," Officer Shuno cut in. Then he turned to Troy and said, "I'll be right back. Stay here." He rushed inside, closing the door behind him.

Moments later, the door creaked open, just enough to allow Chief Creta to poke his head out.

Troy was shocked when he saw the sunken eyes, the hollow face, and the tangled, matted hair.

"Chief Creta!" Troy cried. "Are you all right?" Troy nodded over his shoulder to Bree and Mante, motioning them to come forward. He wanted them to get a good look at the Chief.

But the guards raised their spears and squeezed together, blocking their way.

"What are you doing here, Troy?" the Chief asked in a scratchy voice. "Why aren't you and your friends at the field, where you belong? You're supposed to be building a new fence." He sounded agitated, impatient.

"Then you know about the new fence?" Troy asked, surprised.

"Of course I know about it! I'm the one who ordered it built!"

"*You* ordered it?" Troy asked, stunned. "It was *your* idea?"

"Of course I ordered it!" Chief Creta snapped. "Whose idea did you think it was?" His breathing was labored and he appeared to be getting more tired by the minute.

"Well, I thought maybe Officer Shuno may have ordered it without you even knowing about it," Troy said weakly.

"Officer Shuno was following *my* orders!" the Chief said angrily. "And I expect you and your friends to follow *his* orders! Is that clear?"

Troy was confused. This wasn't the Chief Creta he knew. This Chief wasn't kind and gentle. This Chief was rude and irrational. Something was dreadfully wrong!

"Ah ... yes ... Sir. It's just that I thought ... we thought ... you might consider letting us roll a boulder in front of the new hole in the fence. We think the Spinosaurs will just chew through the new fence. But the boulder would probably stop them. And it would only take about a half a day to—"

"Don't stand there and sass me!" Chief Creta yelled, then lowered his head, coughing violently. When he finished, he said in a weakened voice, "You got your orders—now get to work, all of you."

"But, Sir," Troy cried pleadingly. "We haven't been able to harvest any saltberries for the last two days! The fence will take at least a week to complete—probably longer. And it won't keep the Spinosaurs out anyway!"

Chief Creta looked up at Troy through tired eyes. After clearing his throat, he said, "I don't want to hear another word from you. This is your last warning, lad. Stop being a troublemaker. One more time, and you'll go to the prison tree hut. Do I make myself *emphatically* clear?"

A bird's feather could've knocked Troy over as he stood there, dazed. This wasn't the Chief Creta he knew. He was shocked beyond belief. Only yesterday, Chief Creta had defended him from Officer Shuno's vicious assault. Something was going on here. Something strange. Something ... evil.

"Yes, Sir," Troy said, bewildered and defeated. "You have made yourself very clear. I'm sorry we bothered you."

"Then get out of here and get back to work!" the Chief shouted with frightening authority. "And don't bother me anymore!" Coughing violently again, he jerked his head back inside and slammed the door shut in Troy's face.

The two guards roared with laughter, holding their spears with one hand, and slapping their knees with the other.

Troy was stunned—and angry. He stood staring at the closed door, trying to comprehend what had just happened.

The door opened suddenly, and Officer Shuno stepped out. "Still here?" he asked, his tone devilish. He snapped his fingers, and the tall guard lowered his spear and poked the flint tip against Troy's stomach. "You heard the Chief," he barked. "Now get out of here!"

Bree slipped her hand into Troy's. "Come on, Troy. There's

nothing more we can do here." She led Troy and Mante to the stairs.

As they trudged down, Troy heard Officer Shuno scolding the guards in a hushed voice. "You fools! I told you, it has to look like an accident!"

Chapter 6

When they reached the bottom of the stairs, Bree said, "Where to now?"

"The saltberry field of course," said Mante. "We got a lot of fence to build."

"I don't know," said Bree. "I still like Troy's idea better."

Troy was standing behind them, dazed. His entire body felt weak with anxiety, and his stomach felt queasy.

Bree turned to face him. "What do you think, Tro—" She stopped abruptly, obviously taken aback by his condition."What's wrong? You look like you've just been chased by a pack of Spinosaurs!"

His face puckered, his eyes searching hers. "You didn't hear him?"

"Who?"

"Officer Shuno," Troy answered. "He wants to kill me."

"What are you talking about?" Mante asked, his hands on his hips.

"I just heard Officer Shuno telling his guards to make it look like an accident," said Troy.

"Are you sure?" Bree asked, her face creased with worry.

"Positive," Troy said. "I just overheard him talking to his guards as we were leaving."

"Then I'd say you were right about that Troodon," said Bree. "Officer Shuno probably planted it in your cupboard, just like you said."

"Well, if *that* doesn't tell you you're becoming a nuisance, then I don't know what will," said Mante."And now you even got Chief Creta mad at you."

"You can't go by what Chief Creta just told me," said Troy. "He's never yelled at me before. Obviously he's not himself today. Something's wrong."

"I think you're right, Troy," said Bree. "He's definitely not himself. Chief Creta would never go along with a stupid plan like building an entire new fence. Something is definitely wrong here."

"Oh, brother," Mante said, rolling his eyes. "Not you too!" They ignored his remark.

"Then we have to stay and help the Chief," Troy blurted.

"No," Bree said. "That would be a mistake. We're already outnumbered here. Our only hope of helping the Chief is by convincing the others to help us. Maybe we can convince them of rolling a boulder in front of the hole, too."

"Sure makes more sense than building a whole new fence," Troy said. He turned to Mante and said, "Are you still with us, Mante?"

Mante's face puffed up with anger. "Look, buddy, you almost got us killed today—you and your stupid plan. I told you we didn't need another plan, and I was right. You even heard it straight from Chief Creta's mouth. So count me out. I'm going to work." Mante turned and left in a huff.

Troy was furious. "Sometimes he really ticks me off," he said through his teeth. "I thought we were friends."

"Forget it," Bree said. "We'll do it without him." She grabbed his hand. "Come on, we'd better go. We don't want to get caught hanging around here."

On their way back to the saltberry field, Troy felt a throbbing pain in his stomach. He held his hand over the spot where the guard had poked him with the spear.

"Still hurt?" Bree asked.

"Just a little," said Troy."But I'm more concerned about Chief Creta. I love that old guy. He's like a grandfather to me. I just can't believe he actually yelled at me like that. He must be in a bad way."

"I know," said Bree. "Don't worry, we'll get to the bottom of this."

As they neared the field, Troy happened to see Panga in the forest, a few yards from the path, his head in the tree-tops as usual.

"Come on," said Troy. "I want you to meet a friend of mine." He led her off the path, through the brush, and stopped at Panga's giant feet. "Troy! What are you doing?" Bree cried. "Do you want to get trampled?"

Troy chuckled. "It's okay. He's mine. You're safe." Then he cupped his hands over his mouth, looked up, and yelled. "Hey, Panga! Come say hello! Here, boy!"

The bulky Saltasaur slowly lowered his head to eye level with Troy, chewing on a branch protruding from his mouth. The giant's brown, liquid eyes blinked once, staring at Troy and Bree. He continued munching silently.

"Meet Panga," said Troy, stroking the dinosaur's chin.

"Oh, my gosh!" Bree cried, holding her cheeks. "He's tame!"

"Of course he's tame. Go ahead—pet him."

Timidly, she stroked Panga's head. "He's so sweet. But how did you tame him?"

"I found him four years ago, down by the lake," Troy said. "Some friends and I were swimming one day, and we found Panga's mother—or what was left of her—on the shore.

Spinosaurs got her. I found Panga in the cave right by the shore, near his mother. He was only a baby. His mother must've nudged him into the cave with her nose, before facing the Spinosaurs head-on. Luckily the mouth of the cave is too small for Spinosaurs to get inside. When I found him, Panga was in there all by himself, huddled in a corner, whimpering."

"Awww," said Bree. "The poor thing." She stroked Panga tenderly, lovingly, her timidity completely gone.

"So I brought him home and asked my parents if I could keep him and raise him. And they said okay under one condition."

"What was that?" asked Bree.

"That I never bring him into the house once he's full-grown," Troy said, smiling, then winked at her.

"Oh, you," she said, chuckling. "I get it. Ha! Ha! Ha! Very funny!"

Having finished eating his branch, Panga gently licked Bree's hand.

"He likes you," said Troy.

"Of course he does. Good taste must run in your family."

Troy and Bree looked at each other, held the gaze for just a moment, then burst out laughing.

"Come on," he said. "We'd better get back to the field."

They each gave Panga one last pat, then said goodbye, and continued on their way.

When they arrived at the field, Troy was amazed to see the amount of work the villagers had accomplished while he was gone with Bree and Mante. A good portion of the south end—the end opposite the gate and the adjacent gaping hole—had been completed.

"Wow!" he said, fascinated. "These guys are really going to town. Look how much they got done already!"

"It's unbelievable!" Bree remarked. "Maybe it won't take as long to build as we thought it would. Maybe we should just go along with it and get it over with."

"Except for one thing."

"What's that?"

"Even if we could build the entire new fence in one day, it won't do any good. The Spinosaurs will still chew right through *both* fences. We need a boulder—not a fence."

Troy watched, astonished, as hundreds of villagers worked in harmony in their various groups. Each work group was responsible for a specific job. The cutters were in the surrounding forest, cutting cottonwood trees down with their stone axes.

The pointers were chopping the fallen trees into logs and pointing one end.

The draggers were dragging the pointed logs to the saltberry field, where they stacked them in small piles around the perimeter.

The diggers were carving a trench, just outside the existing fence, barely keeping ahead of the erectors.

The erectors were setting the logs—pointed end first—into the trench, lining them up for the pile drivers.

The pile drivers were pounding the logs securely into place with stone sledge hammers. Theirs was probably the most backbreaking job of all. The bracers were bracing the newly driven logs against the existing fence, with poles that slanted at an angle.

Several diggers were backfilling the trench, shoveling loose dirt against the newly erected logs and firmly tamping it down with the backside of their wooden shovels.

"They're working so hard," Bree said. "But it's all in vain."

"Yeah," said Troy. "And if we don't get a boulder to plug that hole, we're not going to have any saltberries for a very long time."

"We'll starve," said Bree. "Every last one of us."

"Let's go talk to some of these people," said Troy. "If we can convince only about a dozen of them, we can get that boulder in place today."

"Let's start with the cutters," Bree suggested.

As they approached the workers, one of the cutters cupped his hands around his mouth and shouted, "Tim-m-m-ber-r-r-r-r!

An ear-shattering cracking noise ripped through the forest, and a giant cottonwood came smashing down through a maze of smaller trees. Flocks of forest birds exploded from the underbrush, taking to the sky.

Within seconds, the pointers were swarming the fallen tree, hacking away with their axes, lopping off branches and chopping the tree into sections.

Troy walked up to them, dodging small wooden chips that flew in the air as their axes bit into the wood. "Excuse me," he said.

The workers paid him no attention.

Troy spoke a little louder. "Hey, guys! Can I have your attention for a moment?"

Several of them glanced up at him, but they kept right on working.

"Yo, guys!" he shouted. "Gotta talk to ya!"

Some of the workers stopped, looked up at him. Others ignored him.

Troy put two fingers to his mouth and whistled.

Now all the cutters and pointers stopped their work.

Troy stepped up on a fallen log. "Listen, guys. Not only are we wasting trees for nothing, we're wasting valuable time. The Spinosaurs will easily chew through both fences—I'm sure of it. The only thing that will stop them now is a huge boulder wedged in the hole in the fence. But it'll take about a dozen of us to roll it into place. And if we get started now, we could probably still get it done today. And while we're placing the boulder, the rest of the people could be planting a new crop of saltberries."

He studied their faces, searching for the least bit of enthusiasm. But there was none.

He cleared his throat. "Our supply of saltberries is getting very low."

No response.

"So how about it, guys. Can I see some volunteers?"

"Not on your life!" one of the workers snapped. "You've already gotten us into enough of a mess."

Troy was shocked by the sharp remark. What's going on here? he thought. We used to be a happy, peaceful village. Now everyone is becoming downright hostile!

"What do you mean?" Troy asked. "What are you talking about?"

Another worker lashed out. "If you hadn't left that hoe handle sticking out of the fence, we wouldn't be in this fix. It's all your fault!"

"Now wait just a minute!" Bree cried, storming into the group. Her face was tense, fists clenched at her sides. "I think you're treating Troy unfairly. Officer Shuno had no business forcing Troy to stay after dark that night."

Troy was embarrassed by her outburst. "It's okay, Bree," he said, "I'll handle this."

"Don't let them treat you like this, Troy," she said, fire in her eyes. "It's not fair!" She turned on the crowd again. "Can't you see Troy is only trying to help you? Do you people realize you'll probably all starve to death before you finish the new fence? Can't you people see that?"

Another worker spoke up. "Listen, miss, it's like they said. Your friend here is the cause of all this trouble. No offense, but the last thing we need right now is anymore help from him! You both best be on your way now, less you care to pitch in and help us build the fence. You'll not find anyone around here to go along with your plans."

"I can't believe it!" Bree cried. "You're all too ignorant to see what's going on here! You're all going to starve!"

"Now look, miss," the worker said, "I've already tol—"

Troy jumped off the log and grabbed Bree's hand. "Never mind," he interrupted. "We'll go talk to the others. If they feel the same as you guys, we'll give it up and help you build the fence."

The worker shrugged. "Suit yourself, son."

"Come on, Bree. Let's go talk to the diggers and the pile drivers. Maybe we can talk some sense into *them*."

"Don't be getting caught now by Officer Shuno," the worker called after them. "I don't expect he'll take too kindly to you wandering around, talking to the others."

As they walked together, Troy said, "Bree, can I ask you a favor?" His tone was serious.

She looked at him inquisitively. "Sure."

"I know you mean to be helpful, but I really don't like it when you stick up for me in front of the men like that. It's ... well ... you know ... humiliating."

Bree stopped in her tracks. A fire sparked in her eyes, and her face grew red with anger. She turned on him with the ferocity of a wounded Spinosaur. "I can't believe you said that!" she snapped. "After all we've been through these past few days. I thought we were a team."

"We are!"

"Are we? Do team members criticize one another?"

"I'm not criticizing you, Bree. I just don't want you to embarrass me in front of those guys, that's all."

"Yeah, right!"

"Come on, Bree," he pleaded. "It's a guy thing. Don't be mad."

"Forget it, okay?" She was staring straight up at the sky, blinking back tears.

He put his hands on her waist and drew her close. She lowered her head, biting her lip.

Their eyes met.

"You know, getting to know someone who you care about deeply can be a lot of hard work," he said. He brushed a strand of hair off her cheek.

"I care deeply about you, too," she said, sobbing. "That's why it bothers me when those guys treat you so unfairly. I didn't know I was doing anything wrong, sticking up for you." Her tears flowed freely.

He took her in his arms, holding her close. He stroked her hair as he spoke. "Shh. It's okay. Don't cry, Bree. You didn't do anything wrong. I guess I'm just too proud to let my girl stand up for me in front the guys. But I gotta tell you something, girl … "

He lifted her chin. "I care about you. More than anything on this island."

"Oh, Troy," she said, hugging him, "I care about you, too. Very much. I'm sorry I embarrassed you."

"It's okay," he said. "Shh. It's okay. I'm sorry, too. We're going through some pretty tough times right now."

"We are in a jam, aren't we?" she said, trying to compose herself. "Yes, we are, and it's probably going to get tougher. But at least we're together."

"Okay," she said, smiling radiantly, her big green eyes sparkling. "Isn't it weird?"

"What?"

"Well, it seems the closer two people become, it's easier for their feelings to get hurt by one another."

"Yeah, but it's worth it!" he joked.

She chuckled. "How do you do it?"

"What?"

"Cope?"

"What do you mean?"

"Well, first it was your father's death, and now this mess. Practically the whole village is against you. How do you cope with that?"

Troy thought for a moment. "I don't know. I never thought about it before. I guess I just do what I gotta do."

"And that's all there is to it?"

"Well, yeah. I mean, I just get up every morning and go take care of whatever needs taking care of." He frowned. "Of course, some things are out of my hands. Like my dad's death. Nothing I can do about that."

"So every day you just rise and shine and go out and face the world."

"Yeah," said Troy. "What else is there? I mean, that's what you have to do—every day."

"Why?"

"Why! What do you mean, why? I don't know *why*. You just have to, that's all. Because life is like that, I guess. Life is so ... daily."

She gazed at him, her eyes warm and cheerful. "You're good for me," she said, then kissed his nose.

He was beaming. "Right now, I feel like the biggest man on the island."

Troy kept her by his side as he talked to several more groups of workers. But it was all in vain. No one would listen to him. No matter how hard he tried, he could not convince a single person to help him roll a boulder in the gaping hole. By late afternoon, he and Bree had accomplished nothing.

"Serves them right if they all starve to death," he said bitterly.

"Troy!" Bree cried, shocked. "You don't mean that!"

He hung his head. "Of course not. It's just so aggravating. Nobody'll listen. It's almost like they *want* to suffer." He kicked a clump of soil. "I just don't get it."

"There's about an hour left before quitting time," Bree said. "Is there anything we can do before we go home? Maybe we should just start helping them with the fence."

"Sure! Why not?" he said sarcastically. "We'll go and help the fools build their stupid fence, and then we can all sit around and watch each other starve. Won't that be fun?"

She fired a glance at him, her eyes narrowed.

He backed off immediately when he saw the fire in her eyes. "I'm sorry. I didn't mean that."

"So what'll we do?" she asked, no longer annoyed.

"I know!"

"What?"

"Well," said Troy, "we already know that everyone will be running out of saltberries long before the fence is finished."

"Right."

"And every tree hut on the island has a porch."

"So?"

"And every porch has a railing, and every railing has a long, built-in flower box."

"So what?"

"So we go to the storage tree hut and get some saltberry seeds to take home with us. Then we plant the seeds in our flower boxes!"

Bree shook her head in amazement. "You're incredible!" she said, smiling. "How in the world do you come up with this stuff?"

Encouraged, he began bubbling with new excitement.

"And we can post a note at the gate, telling the others to do the same!"

His enthusiasm was contagious. "Yeah!" Bree said. "Everyone can grow their own berries at home, until the fence is finished!"

Troy felt proud of his idea. "At least no one will starve to death."

Her face became serious. "But what if they refuse to plant the berries?"

"Well, we can't force them. But don't worry—after they get good and hungry, they'll use the flower boxes."

"But we haven't any parchment here, nothing to write on."

"No," he said, "I'll have to write the note tonight at my hut, and then post it first thing tomorrow morning. Meanwhile, let's get our own seeds out of the shed, and go home and plant them."

Later, he kissed her goodbye at the foot of her stairs, the two of them holding leather sacks of saltberry seeds. "See you tomorrow," he said, then kissed her again. "And don't forget to plant those seeds."

"Okay. Goodbye, Troy. See you tomorrow. I ... love you."

"I love you, too!" As he headed home, he could barely contain himself, he was so excited.

A short while later, Troy arrived at his tree hut and began to climb the winding stairs. Suddenly, a wooden step collapsed beneath him. He plunged forward and smashed into the steps above. But those steps, too, collapsed. In a frenzy, he clawed at anything he could hold onto, his fingers like talons, groping furiously for a handhold.

At the last possible instant, he locked onto a solid step above him. His body dangled through the opening, high above the forest floor. His legs swung to and fro, weakening his grip. Soon his hands went numb.

Can't hold on! his mind screamed. Have to swing my feet up!

He closed his eyes and gritted his teeth. Using every ounce of his strength, he pulled himself up, until his chin was level with the first solid step. He thrust his chin between his hands, gasping, and clamped it down on the stair. Then, using his chin and both hands, he pulled with all his might. Slowly, painfully, he raised himself. Finally, he was able to raise himself high enough to prop an elbow on the step—first one, and then the other. Then he desperately lifted himself the rest of the way, the seed bag hanging safely around his neck from a shoulder strap.

Panting heavily and drenched in sweat, he stared in horror at the jagged opening, where only a moment before, he had stood. A sickening sensation washed over him and he shuddered violently, as he recalled Officer Shuno's words: "Make it look like an accident."

Chapter 7

Troy warned his mom of the broken stairs, and she was beside herself.

"When does it stop!" she cried, clutching her stomach. "I can't take much more of this." She sat on a stool at the kitchen table. "Maybe I should just go over there myself and demand to speak to Chief Creta. He'll listen to *me*."

Troy became alarmed. "No, Ma, don't even think about it. Officer Shuno has already threatened to throw you in the prison tree hut, too. Remember?"

"Then what? There must be something we can do to stop this madness!"

Troy filled her in on his plan to post a note at the field, instructing everyone to plant saltberries in their flower boxes.

"Well, that's a start," said his mom. "Then at least no one will starve."

And eventually, I'm sure everyone will come around and see how pointless it is to build the fence," Troy added. "Then maybe they'll help me roll a boulder and plug that hole once and for all."

"Well, you be careful," his mom warned. "And stay out of Officer Shuno's way—whatever you do." She stood up and pushed the stool back under the table. "I'll tell you one thing—I'm keeping our door locked from now on." She went to the plank counter and ladled herself a cup of water from the water pail. "It's a pretty sad day when we have to start locking our doors—something none of us on this island has ever had to do before. Ever." She took a long drink.

"I know," said Troy. "In fact, I'm gonna add an extra bolt on the door before I go to bed tonight."

"Well, don't stay up too late. You need your rest."

"I won't. I'm gonna plant these seeds first, and then I'll do the bolt. I won't fix the stairs until tomorrow morning, when there's more daylight." He grabbed the bag of seeds and headed for the door. "Sorry I have to ruin your flowers."

"Oh, that's okay." His mom finished her water and set the cup down. "Those are only castor-oil plants. Their flowers aren't much to look at anyway. You do whatever you have to do, Troy. I trust you." Then she padded barefoot down the hallway toward her room. "Goodnight, son. I love you."

"Love you, too," he called after her, then stepped outside onto the porch.

Troy went to the wooden flower box and began pulling out the castor-oil plants and tossing them over the railing. When he had finished pulling and tossing the last plant, he noticed that some of them had landed on the ground below, and some of them had gotten hung up in the upper branches of his tree, where they dangled harmlessly. Oh, well, he thought, eventually the wind will knock them down. They won't hurt anything.

When he finished planting the saltberry seeds, he turned his attention to the door bolt. It didn't take him long to fashion a new one from a hunk of oak from the box of firewood in the kitchen. He placed the new bolt a few inches below the existing one, making the door to his hut twice as strong.

Having finished his chores, he went to bed and, in spite of his stressful day—or maybe because of it—he slept peacefully for the first time in days.

* * *

The next morning Troy arose early to allow himself time to harvest the saltberries from the flower box, sit down to a breakfast of fried saltberries, and repair the stairs before rushing off to Bree's.

When he stepped outside to pick the berries, Panga was already there, grazing in the treetop. "Good morning, Panga," Troy said, smiling, then remembered he had forgotten to pick fern branches for Panga the day before. "Sorry, boy," he said. "I did it again, but I'll get you some as soon as I finish fixing the stairs."

Panga lowered his head from the branches, nuzzled Troy's cheek with his nose, then returned to grazing.

Troy watched him as he devoured tree branches and the dangling castor oil plants alike. "Save some room for your fern treats," Troy said, chuckling.

After harvesting the saltberries, Troy was pleased with himself for being able to provide for himself and his mom. Since the flower box was only a foot wide by four feet long, his harvest was small—only eight berries.

"But eight berries every day is enough to sustain us for a long time," said his mom. "You did a good job, Troy," she said, fixing their breakfast. "I'm proud of you. Your dad would be proud of you, too."

After breakfast, Troy went outside to repair the broken steps.

When the last one had been replaced, he wanted to check them for strength. Grabbing hold of the railing on either side, he bounced, letting his feet land hard on each of the new steps.

The stairs didn't budge. His repairs were more than adequate.

At the bottom of the stairway, he searched for remnants of the broken stairs. He didn't have to look for long; they were scattered on top of the leaf litter that blanketed the forest floor. He gathered the broken pieces and slowly made his way back to the path.

Sitting on the bottom stair, he examined the first fragment. Even though he half-expected to find what he saw, he became unglued, nevertheless. A sickening feeling filled his gut. Deeply scored on the underside were numerous cuts.

Clearly, they had been made with the flint blade of a hatchet.

Just then, Troy heard a tremendous wretching sound erupt in the brush a few feet from where he sat. He jumped up and scurried around the base of his tree and found Panga gagging on something, his head hovering only a foot above the ground, his eyes alarmed and bulging.

"Panga!" cried Troy. "What's wrong, boy? Are you all right?"

Panga paid no attention to Troy, as the ailing Saltasaur continued gagging and coughing.

Troy placed his arms around the gentle giant's neck and hugged him, feeling completely helpless. "Panga! What's wrong?"

Suddenly an enormous burst of vomit erupted from Panga's mouth, spraying the ground and surrounding brush with a thick, blue-green slime.

Troy jumped back, alarmed, and just as a wave of panic was about to wash over him, Panga shuddered violently, then raised his head and returned to grazing in the treetop.

Puzzled, Troy knelt down and examined the puddle of vomit. Mixed in with the blue-green slime were bits of castor-oil plant that Panga had inadvertently eaten while it was hanging from a tree branch.

The castor-oil plant made him sick, Troy thought, spooning through the slime with a stick. It must be poisonous!

Troy walked over to Panga and patted his thick, trunk-like leg. "You all right, boy?" he called, staring up at the dinosaur.

Panga paid him no attention as he continued grazing in the treetop.

Satisfied, Troy climbed the stairs to his tree hut, printed his note about planting saltberries in the flower boxes, and stuffed the parchment into his leather shirt pocket, for posting later at the saltberry field. He kissed his mom good-bye, told her to lock the door, then headed over to Bree's.

When he arrived at Bree's tree hut, she greeted him on her porch. He practically burst with the chilling news of the broken stairs and the telltale hatchet marks.

"That's sabotage with the intent to commit murder!" Bree blurted. "So you were right about Officer Shuno all along."

"Yes," said Troy. "That lunatic wants me dead!"

Then Troy told her about the castor-oil plant and Panga's vomiting.

As he spoke, Bree stared at the flower box along her porch railing. When he finished, she said, "The castor-oil plant must be extremely poisonous to make a full-grown Saltasaur sick." Her eyes were still glued to the box.

"Yeah," said Troy. "And luckily he didn't eat more than he did, or it might've killed him. The good news is, I was able to harvest some saltberries from my flower box this morning!" He noticed her trance-like state and followed her gaze to the flower box. Then he noticed something that shocked and surprised him.

The flower box sported an assortment of wildflowers in various colors. A smattering of weeds grew in green tufts between some of the blossoms. But there were no saltberries. None.

"You didn't plant any berries!" Troy cried.

She looked at him, her face sober. "Troy, I have to talk to you."

"That doesn't sound good," said Troy, a sense of dread working its way into the pit of his stomach.

She bit her lip, looking down, avoiding eye contact.

"What is it, Bree?" he asked, the feeling of dread beginning to grow. She looked at him, her eyes glistening with tears. "My parents don't want me to see you anymore." Her voice cracked and her lips trembled. "We have to break off our relationship."

Troy fell back against the porch railing as though a giant oak had just smashed into him. His heart was hammering, as blood rushed to his head. He took a deep breath, cleared his throat. "Why?"

"My father flew into a rage when I told him about your plan to plant saltberries in the flower boxes."

"But it worked!" cried Troy. "My mom and I had some this morning—from our flower box!"

"I knew it would work, Troy. I believe in you. But my dad says you're going against Officer Shuno's orders, and you're going to get into serious trouble if you don't knock it off." She sniffled and wiped her tears. "He says I'll get into trouble, too, just by hanging around with you."

"That's nonsense!" Troy blurted. "Officer Shuno never said we couldn't plant saltberries in our flower boxes."

She sniffled. "No, but he didn't say we could, either. My dad says you should've gotten Officer Shuno's permission first. He says you're deliberately going out of your way to cause trouble, because you want to prove to the whole village what a big man you are."

The initial shock of losing Bree was trickling into anger. "Your dad said that?"

She nodded, her eyes red and swollen.

He frowned, his anger mounting.

"My dad says the whole village is against you, and nobody will ever go along with your plan to plant the seeds in flower boxes because they won't do anything against Officer Shuno because he's the Second Commanding Officer, and it's their responsibility to do whatever he commands. My dad says you're only wasting your time by posting your note at the field."

"The note!" Troy cried, patting his shirt pocket. "I've got to get the note posted before everyone arrives at the field. Hopefully they'll read it first thing this morning, and then take some seeds home with them to plant tonight. By tomorrow morning, everyone will have berries to pick."

She stopped her sniffling and stared at him. "Have you heard a word I just said?"

"I heard," he said. "But that was your dad talking, not you." He put his arms around her, his eyes searching hers. "Right?"

She quickly averted her eyes. "What if he's right?" she asked, fidgeting with her fingers. "What if my dad is right?"

She looked up at him, waiting for his response.

"He's wrong. Dead wrong." His tone was cold and callous.

Shocked, she pushed herself away from him. "That's easy for you to say, Troy. But he's my father, and I can't go against him."

"No, no, no! We wouldn't want to go against Daddy, would we?" he said sarcastically.

Her face flashed with anger and bitterness. "Don't start running down my father!" she snapped.

"Don't worry, I wouldn't *think* of it."

"Good! Then I guess there's nothing more for us to discuss."

"No, I guess not." He turned to leave, then stopped and faced her. "Oh, I almost forgot. Could you scrape some pail-putty from one of your water pails and give it to me?"

She looked at him, bewildered. "What for?"

"I need it to stick it on my note so I can post it on the gate at the field. I forgot to bring some from home."

Rolling her eyes, she stormed inside, then marched back out, carrying a pebble-sized ball of putty. "Here!" she said, jabbing it at him.

He took it from her and placed it inside his shirt pocket, next to his note. "Thanks."

"You're still going to go through with it?" she asked, her voice softer now. "In spite of everything I've told you, you're still going to post your note?"

"I have to. I can't let everyone on this island starve to death, while Officer Shuno sits in the town hall playing Second Commanding Officer. I *know* he's up to something. I *know* there's something wrong with Chief Creta. And I *know* Officer Shuno is behind it."

"But you don't know *what* he's up to."

"No, I don't." He looked at her squarely. "But I'm gonna find out."

"But you're all alone. No one believes you. No one trusts you."

He hesitated, silently gazing at her.

The silence between them was louder than the forest birds trilling in nearby treetops.

Finally, he spoke. "I thought *you* believed me, trusted me."

Her eyes filled with tears again. "I do believe you, Troy. And, yes, I do trust you. But I can't go against my parents. Can't you see that? Right or wrong, I have to do what they tell me. I have to obey them—just like all of us have to obey Officer Shuno."

"I don't expect you to disobey your parents, Bree. I really don't. They're good people. They're only trying to protect you. I don't blame them, but I hope you can change their minds." He touched her cheek. "I'm gonna miss you."

Her lips began trembling. "I'm going to miss you, too," she sobbed. "Be careful, and—" Her voice spiralled into a squeak, cut off by her crying.

A lump throbbed in his throat, and he felt his own eyes beginning to mist.

* * *

Upon arriving at the saltberry field, Troy used the pail-putty to post his note on the gate. He read it carefully, one last time, to make sure it sounded just right:

Attention everyone:
   Due to the shortage of saltberries, it is important that you take home some saltberry seeds today, and plant them in your flower boxes. If you don't have a flower box, come see me and I'll build one for you.
   Sincerely, Troy.

Satisfied, he began walking along the exterior perimeter of the fence, inspecting the new construction. Just as he had expected, the Spinosaurs hadn't bothered the fence last night. Why would they? he thought. There aren't any berries planted in the field, and the hole they had previously chewed hasn't been patched again, yet. The Spinosaurs can still come and go, in and out of the field, if they wanted to.

After inspecting the fence, Troy wondered what he should do next. I might as well help the others with the construction, he thought. Nothing else I can do now.

He pondered a moment, trying to decide which job function he would perform. Guess I'll be a chopper, he thought. Only takes one person to chop down a tree. I can get started now, even though there's no one else here.

By the time he had fetched an axe from the storage tree hut, other people were beginning to arrive at the field. He watched with pride as they gathered around his note. He heard them chattering excitedly.

The group of curious workers grew larger, and soon a small crowd was huddled around his note, their backs to him.

Whistling, he walked past them, out through the gate, and into the nearby forest to chop down a tree.

I'll pick one that's already dead, he thought. No sense in wasting a live tree. The Spinosaurs will only chew through it anyway.

His search for a dead tree led him deeper and deeper into the forest. When he reached a dark, dank, secluded area, he found a giant dead cypress that jutted up from the forest floor, its smooth, weather-beaten trunk stretching straight up before exploding into a tangled mass of bare, snarly branches. The green live branches of neighboring trees created a thick, almost impenetrable canopy that blocked most of the sun's rays.

Should be able to get several good logs from this one, he thought.

He tucked the axe under one arm, spit into his palms, then briskly rubbed his hands together. Then he picked up the axe and swung it hard. The sharp flint blade bit into the tree, spraying the immediate area with wooden chips. He swung again and again, slowly gouging a wedge-shaped cut.

His chopping was interrupted when, from the corner of his eye, he saw a Spinosaur, partially hidden in the underbrush, staring at him through red, slit-like eyes.

The beast didn't budge or make a sound. It stood stock-still, its sail of spines bristling above its massive head, staring through a tangle of branches. It was so close, Troy could smell its foul breath.

Troy's heart practically jumped into his throat, banging furiously.

Terrified, he didn't know what to do. Trying to think straight, he decided it would be wise to put some distance between them. Slowly he raised one foot off the ground, still clutching the axe.

The Spinosaur instantly cocked its enormous head, never taking its eyes off of Troy's.

Troy stepped back carefully. A twig cracked beneath his foot.

The monster's head snapped up, its eyes widening.

Troy lifted his other foot up off the ground and slowly took another step backwards. As he moved, the creature's eyes followed him.

He took another step back.

Then another, the axe held out in front of him.

The beast let its tooth-studded jaw drop open. Saliva drooled between its dagger-like teeth and dripped on the ground.

Another step back.

It cocked its head to the other side.

Another step.

The nostrils flared open and a tremendous rush of air blasted from them, creating a long, loud hissing noise.

Troy shivered.

Another step.

The giant lowered its head, but its eyes stayed glued to Troy's.

Suddenly the monstrous jaws popped wide open, emitting an earsplitting, bloodcurdling shriek that reverberated throughout the surrounding forest.

Forest birds burst from the treetops, squawking and cackling, flying away in a frenzy.

Troy stumbled and fell backwards.

Still clutching the axe, he scrambled to his feet, heart hammering, blood rushing to his head, knees turning into water.

The beast charged.

Branches cracked and splintered as the Spinosaur crashed through the underbrush. It was upon Troy in a flash, standing over him, blasting him with an earshattering roar.

Troy ducked behind a tree, just as the monster's jaws snapped shut only inches from where his face had been.

It snapped again, viciously biting and tearing at the tree trunk. It spat out a huge chunk of bark, then resumed its attack on Troy.

Troy didn't have time to swing the axe. Instead, he jabbed it into the snapping jaws.

The axe blade disappeared inside the giant mouth. The jaws slammed shut around the axe handle, biting it in half as easily as if it had been a twig.

Seeing his only weapon destroyed, Troy turned and ran. Smacking into a tree with several lower branches, he shot up the tree, expecting the Spinosaur to nip off a foot before he could reach safety. His mind raced with terror, his thinking scrambled. This can't be happening! They only come out at night!

His nerves were frayed, draining him of physical strength. When he reached the top, and could climb no more, he clung to the tapered trunk with all his might. As he caught his breath, he realized why the beast was out during the day. Because I stumbled on its day bed, he thought. They have to go somewhere during the day—into the deep, secluded woods to sleep.

His heart skipped a beat when another terrifying thought flashed inside his brain: There could be more!

He clung to the treetop. The only sound was that of his blood coursing, pounding in his ears.

There was no sign of the Spinosaur.

It's gone! he thought hopefully.

Then he heard a terrible gagging sound, somewhere below, away from the tree. He strained to look out beyond the branches, bending some out of the way. And then he saw it.

The huge creature was standing in a small clearing. It was shaking its head savagely from side to side. Its great spined sail bristled with each thrust of its head. It was choking on something.

Then Troy saw it—the severed end of his axe handle, protruding from the monster's mouth. It was stuck, and the giant beast was trying desperately to dislodge it.

Its hacking grew louder. Then the wounded Spinosaur dropped suddenly to its knees, then crashed to the ground. Its breath blasted from flared nostrils, and blew puffs of dust up from the ground, like small clouds of smoke. It jerked its head up, eyes rolling back, then slammed back down into the ground, its body convulsing.

Finally, the gigantic Spinosaur lay still, its eyes staring lifelessly.

Chapter 8

The next morning, Troy was in high spirits, in spite of his frightening experience only yesterday. He had been so unnerved by the Spinosaur attack, he had gone straight home for the remainder of the day.

And when he had told his mom about the close call, she had almost fainted, having collapsed on the floor. He had revived her by fanning her and giving her a cup of water. She had cried and wailed, and he had felt bad for her, having watched her relive the torment she had suffered when his dad had been killed by a Spinosaur two years ago. "It won't happen again, Ma," he had promised her. "I'll never go that deep into the woods ever again."

The rest of that day had been sober and depressing. He had feared for her health—both mental and physical. Dad's death really took a lot out of her, he had thought. And then he had realized that it had taken a lot out of him, as well. Finally, he had fallen asleep, completely spent.

But this morning Troy was feeling cheerful because he had woken up to an entire flower box full of saltberries, having planted them the day before. Again there were only eight of them, but it was plenty for him and his mom.

I even have enough to pack for lunch today, he thought. And I can save some for seeds.

Later, he would scoop some seeds out of some berries and set them in the sun to dry. Thus, a continual supply of seeds and berries would be forthcoming.

And then there's always the chance that some of the villagers ignored my note and didn't plant any for themselves, he thought. In that case, I'll be needing a lot more saltberries to share with the others.

After breakfast, he went outside and picked some fern branches for Panga. Then, in keeping with tradition, he climbed back upstairs and fed Panga through his bedroom window.

Soon it was time to go to the field, but first he had to promise his mom all over again that he would keep himself safe and out of harm's way. Then, after kissing her good-bye, he headed out, toting a leather sack of fresh saltberries for lunch.

When he arrived at the saltberry field, he noticed that his note was no longer posted. Apparently someone had removed it. I hope they left it up long enough for everyone to read, he thought.

He trudged up the winding stairs to the storage tree hut to get his tools, wondering what job function he would perform today. Think I'll be an erector, he thought. Then I can stay close—real close—to the fence.

He envisioned the dead Spinosaur lying in the woods, the broken axe protruding from its jaws.

He shuddered at the thought.

Inside the storage tree hut, he gathered a coil of rope, a shovel, and a stone sledge hammer.

As he climbed back down, he scanned the saltberry field below. Lying in the field, was nothing but plain, brown dirt.

Usually the field would've been a giant blanket of white, fuzzy saltberries. But because the new fence was nowhere near completion, and the Spinosaurs could still come and go at will in and out of the field, there was no point in planting any berries until the fence was finished.

Not that a new fence will keep them out anyway, Troy thought. I still say we need a boulder, instead. Then we could start planting again.

He reached the bottom of the stairs and thought, I hope they at least planted seeds in their flower boxes last night. Then he started out across the field.

Scattered all along the perimeter of the field were hundreds of workers, already busy at work, constructing the new fence. Troy was shocked to see that their progress had slowed considerably. I don't get it, he thought. They started out so well.

When he plodded away from the cool shade of the storage tree, out into the hot, glaring sun, perspiration beaded along his forehead and dripped into his eyes. No wonder they're slowing down, he thought. With this hot sun and very little food to eat, it's a wonder they don't collapse.

He spent the morning working alongside his fellow villagers, anxiously awaiting lunchtime. He had tried to strike up a conversation with those around him, but every time, they simply grunted or didn't acknowledge him at all.

The cold shoulder treatment, he thought, hoisting a log into place. So this is how they show their gratitude. Nice. Real nice.

Lunchtime finally arrived, and everyone broke from work, scrambling for the shady trees outside the fence. Some of them carried lunch pouches filled with saltberries. Many of them did not.

Troy seized the lunch break as an opportunity to search for Bree in the crowd. As he searched, he removed a saltberry from his leather lunch bag and began munching on it. I miss her so much, he thought. More than I ever thought possible. Maybe I can have lunch with her—if her parents aren't around.

As he walked along, looking for Bree, he saw Mante sitting alone. "Mante! How's it going?" he cried, happy to see his friend. Mante looked up. "Oh … hi, Troy," he said flatly.

Troy was offended by Mante's lack of enthusiasm. "I know you're glad to see me, but try not to get so emotional about it," he kidded.

Mante didn't look up, didn't answer. He was sitting with his back to a tree, his knees drawn up, his arms wrapped around his legs.

Troy frowned. "What's eating you?"

Mante glanced up at him, then looked away. "Nothing."

"Have you seen Bree around?"

"I saw her yesterday," Mante said, staring at the ground between his feet. "We ate lunch together. But I haven't seen her today."

The reply sliced through him like a dagger. He felt his blood begin to boil with jealousy, but he didn't want to give Mante that satisfaction. Controlled, he said, "That's why *I'm* looking for her … to have lunch with her."

"Hmmp!" Mante scoffed. "You'll never find her in *this* crowd. Lunch will be over by the time you find her. Besides, I thought you were supposed to stay away from her."

Troy gritted his teeth. "She told you that?"

"Yeah, during lunch yesterday. She says her father thinks you're a troublemaker."

"Does she feel that way about me, too?" Troy asked, his tone grave.

Mante looked up at him, shocked. "Are you crazy? Don't you know how that girl feels about you?"

Troy perked up, burning with curiosity. "What did she say?"

"Oh, nothing much. She just brags about you the whole time, that's all. I'll tell you one thing buddy ... that girl is really stuck on you." He picked a blade of grass and began shredding it with his fingers, staring out across the field. "I just wish she had felt that way about me."

Troy felt bad for his friend, but the elation he felt for Bree far surpassed any sympathy he had for Mante. Beaming, he said, "I'm gonna go find her, have lunch with her. Thanks a lot, Mante. See ya later."

"Whoa! Hold on there, buddy. I don't think you'd better try to find her today. I saw her parents here. She's probably eating lunch with them right now."

Troy's enthusiasm vanished. "I can't visit with her if her parents are around."

"No," said Mante. "If her dad sees you talking to her, you might get her into trouble."

"Yeah, you're right," Troy said. Frustrated, he kicked a clump of dirt, spraying loose soil into the surrounding grass.

"I think you should put off seeing her until her parents aren't around."

"Yeah, but when will that ever be?" Troy asked. "She's always with her folks."

"Well," said Mante, "you'll just have to meet her someplace, sometime."

"Yeah!" Troy cried, his face filled with new excitement. "That's it!"

"What?"

"A rendezvous!"

"What?"

"You know ... a secret meeting place! I'll write Bree a note telling her where and when to meet me, and *you* can deliver it for me."

"Uh, wait a minute, Troy. I don't wannna get mixed up in this."

"What do you mean? What's the big deal? You just hand her the note and forget about it."

Mante's face was grim. "Look, I already saved your skin *once* from your stupid note-writing. I'm *not* going to get involved *this* time," Mante said sternly.

"What are you talking about?" Troy asked, frowning.

"Your note by the gate ... I took it down."

Shocked, Troy stared at him. "What'd you do that for?" he yelled, his hands on his hips.

"To save your hide, that's what for!" Mante snapped.

"You had no right to do that! I thought you were my friend!"

"I *am* your friend. That's why I did it. I saw Officer Shuno coming down the path yesterday, heading for the field. I knew if he saw your note, he'd be all over you, but good. So I tore the note down before he arrived at the gate."

"You had no right to do that!"

"Look, buddy!" Mante barked. "I saved your behind. He would've thrown you into prison for sure, if he had seen your note."

Troy noticed that the workers sitting in the grass around him were watching him and Mante, their tired faces staring up at them. They're supposed to be eating lunch, he thought. But they're not. They don't even have lunch pouches with them.

"I left that note there for these people. I'm trying to keep them from starving. You should've left the note alone, you fool!"

There was a rush of gasps and murmurs from the huddled workers.

Mante sprang to his feet. "I didn't remove your note

until after everyone had arrived yesterday," he said, his voice cold and hard. "They all read your stupid note, but they chose to ignore it. Nobody is going to follow your ideas anymore. You're not in charge—Officer Shuno is. And nobody wants to get into trouble with *him*. I think we would all rather tangle with a Spinosaur than with Officer Shuno."

The remark reminded Troy of the Spinosaur attack the day before, and he told Mante all about it.

Mante gasped, as did the other workers who were sitting close enough to hear the story.

"You see!" cried Mante. "You've got enough problems already. The last thing you need is to mess with Officer Shuno. Trust me—I did you a big favor by taking your note down."

Troy was exasperated. He felt like pulling his hair out. "Don't you get it?" he asked Mante. "It's because of Officer Shuno that I was almost killed yesterday. If I hadn't been in the woods, cutting down a tree for that stupid fence, following Officer Shuno's stupid orders, I wouldn't have been attacked in the first place. That idiot is going to get us all killed—one way or another."

The workers nearby gasped, and a rush of chattering erupted among them.

Mante suddenly grabbed Troy's arm and whispered, "Are you nuts! You can't talk that way about Officer Shuno. He's the Second Commanding Officer!"

Troy broke loose from Mante's grip. "I don't care who he is. And I'm not the one who's nuts—Officer Shuno is!" He looked at the workers around him who were still chattering excitedly, their hollow faces expressing shock.

"Why aren't they eating?" he asked Mante, nodding at them. "We don't have any berries left," Mante said. "We've eaten our reserve supply."

Troy turned on the surrounding workers. "Why didn't you people plant a crop in your flower boxes?" he exploded.

The tired, hungry workers hung their heads in silence.

"I warned you!" Troy went on, his hands curled into fists. "All of you! Now what will you eat? How will you survive? The fence won't be done for weeks. Can't you see? You'll all starve!"

"We'll manage," Mante said calmly.

Troy looked at him incredulously. "Manage! How?"

Mante faced him, his manner cool and uncaring. "The fence will be done soon, and then we'll—"

"But it won't be done soon," Troy interrupted. "Look around. It's not even halfway built. At the rate we're going, it'll take weeks to build it. How in the world do you all expect to survive if you don't plant any berries until then?"

The workers were gaping at him, but they remained silent.

"None of us is starving yet," Mante said confidently, running his hands through his hair. "Besides, we all have plenty of honey to eat."

Troy looked around him at the huddled workers. "I don't see anyone eating honey. I don't see anyone eating *anything*."

"Nobody brings the honey to the field," said Mante. "It's too awkward, too messy. What we're doing is rationing the stuff. Everyone has agreed to eat only two spoonfuls in the morning and two spoonfuls at night. It isn't much, but it'll keep us from starving for a while."

"And when the honey is gone, then what?" Troy demanded angrily.

"We can always collect more honey in the woods," Mante said simply. Troy frowned, shaking his head in disgust. "This whole thing is so stupid! So unnecessary. You're all suffering from hunger and exhaustion, and there's no reason for it. All you have to do is at least plant some berries in your flower boxes at home. Meanwhile, some of us could get busy on that boulder. We could have that hole in the fence plugged in one day. And we could have the entire field planted again within a day. All I need is about a dozen volunteers."

He stared intently at the workers, searching their eyes, waiting for a reply. But as his gaze met theirs, they quickly averted their eyes and remained silent.

"Forget it," Mante said. "Nobody's going to listen to you. Nobody's going to go against Officer Shuno's orders. Give it up, buddy."

"No, I won't give it up!" Troy cried. "Not until I convince these people that Officer Shuno is not fit to be our leader. He's mentally unfit and we shouldn't be following his orders about *anything!*"

Another rush of gasps erupted among the workers. They stared at Troy, shocked.

Mante grabbed Troy's shoulders, his face wild. "For crying out loud, Troy … keep quiet!"

"No, I won't keep quiet. I'm only speaking the truth, and you know it!"

"Do you have any idea what Officer Shuno would do if one of these people tattled on you?" Mante whispered.

"Let them tattle. I'm only trying to help them. You're all going to—"

"No, we're *not* going to starve to death," Mante interrupted. "We'll make it. We'll be fine. You're worrying for nothing. We'll plant the saltberries in time. None of us has starved yet. In fact, Mr. and Mrs. Droma are the only ones having a problem."

"Mr. and Mrs. Droma!" Troy cried. "They're my next door neighbors!"

"I know."

"What's wrong with them?"

Mante's face became sober. "It's their baby girl. They're completely out of saltberries, so they're feeding her honey. But she won't eat the honey. She keeps throwing it up. She must be pretty sick because Mr. Droma didn't come to work today."

Troy tore free from Mante's grasp. "Is that what it'll take to get you people to listen to me?" he shouted. "Does a little baby girl have to starve first before you all come to your senses?" He stormed through the group of sitting workers and headed toward the dirt path.

"Where are you going?" Mante called after him.

"To the Dromas," he called back. "I've got plenty of berries I can share with them, and I'm giving some to their baby—before it's too late!"

"But your work!" Mante shouted. "You can't just walk off the job. It's not quitting time!"

Troy stopped and turned to face Mante. "Watch me!" he said boldly. Then he turned and marched away.

✳ ✳ ✳

Having first stopped at home to get more berries, Troy now climbed the winding stairs to the Dromas' tree hut. He carried the life-sustaining saltberries in a wooden pail, filled to the brim.

As he approached the top, he could hear the baby's screams. Her tiny body must be racked with hunger pains, he thought. He rapped hard on the wooden frame that outlined the thatched door.

No answer.

He knocked again, louder. No answer.

This time he banged with a closed fist.

A moment later, the door opened, and the baby's wailing was suddenly ear-shattering.

Mr. Droma stood in the doorway, one hand cupped around his ear. He was a tall, skinny man with rounded shoulders. Though he was only middle-aged, he appeared to be much older. His face was thin and drawn, and dark circles ran deeply beneath his eyes. Troy had spoken to him enough times in the past to know that he was kind and gentle.

Behind Mr. Droma, Troy could see Mrs. Droma sitting in a chair, holding her baby on her lap. She was holding a spoonful of honey up to the baby's mouth, coaxing her to eat.

But the infant was squirming and crying frantically. The honey was smeared on her small pink face, running down her chin. Her hands flailed with each earsplitting wail.

"Hello, Mr. Droma," Troy said. He spoke loud enough so his voice would carry above the baby's screaming. "I heard about the trouble you were having with your baby, so I brought over some berries." He held the full pail up, smiling.

Mr. Droma was taken aback by the kind gesture, for he stood speechless. Slowly, he took the bucket from Troy, his eyes welling with tears. "Thank you, Troy," he said, his voice cracking. "Thank you very much." Clutching the pail to his chest, he stepped back out of the doorway and said, "Please come in."

Troy stepped inside, feeling somewhat awkward. The tree hut was filled with the baby's spastic screaming. "Been a long time since I've been in here," he said, glancing around. "Not since your little boy fell through the old stair railing and I made you a new one. By the way, how's little Tyran doing?"

"Oh, he's fine," said Mr. Droma. "His broken leg healed completely—thanks to Dr. Hadro. Right now he's in the other room, taking a nap, if you can believe it. How that kid can sleep through this racket is beyond me."

Troy chuckled, then followed Mr. Droma across the room and stood before Mrs. Droma and their infant daughter.

Holding up the pail of berries, Mr. Droma said, "Look, honey! Look what Troy has brought for our little girl!"

Her face exploded with excitement. She practically jumped from her chair, shoved the baby into Mr. Droma's arms, snatched the pail from him, then scurried to the kitchen.

A moment later, she returned with a bowl of mashed saltberries. Sitting in her chair, the bowl in her lap, she reached out to Mr. Droma for the baby. He handed her the screaming infant, and she began feeding her at once.

The baby girl stopped her crying with the first mouthful of food. Eagerly she ate the juicy mush, slurping spoonful after spoonful.

"How can we ever thank you, Troy?" Mrs. Droma asked, looking up at him, her eyes glistening. "She would've died—" Her voice broke off.

Troy cleared his throat. "It's okay, Mrs. Droma," he said, placing a hand on her shoulder. "She'll be all right now. I got plenty of berries at home. I'll bring you some every day until the field gets planted again."

The baby cooed softly as she swallowed another spoonful, her tiny chin smeared with saltberry juice.

Troy stroked her hair. "What's her name?"

"Cera," replied Mrs. Droma, smiling warmly.

Good thing I planted the seeds when I did, Troy thought, beaming with pride. Then he said, "Mr. Droma?"

"Yes?"

Troy cleared his throat again. "Did you happen to read my note posted at the gate?"

"Yes, I did ... yesterday."

"But you still didn't plant any berries?"

Mr. Droma's face became clouded, grim. "No, I didn't."

"Why not?"

Mr. Droma folded his arms across his chest, looking down at his wife. "We're not about to go against Officer Shuno's orders, Troy. No good could ever come of that."

Troy's mouth dropped open, staring disbelievingly at Mr. Droma. "No good could ever come out of what?"

"Disobeying Officer Shuno."

Troy's eyebrows drew together, his face pinched and growing warm. "Where do you think *those* berries came from?" he said, pointing to the bowl in Mrs. Droma's lap.

Mr. Droma hesitated, glanced at his wife.

She looked up at him, shrugged, then looked down at her baby.

Mr. Droma looked at Troy, met his eyes. "Look, Troy. We're very grateful for what you've done, but we can't get involved with this."

"All I need you to do is help me convince the others to plant berries in their flower boxes. That's all. You've seen for yourselves how my idea was a good one. Most of the others are already out of saltberries. If I hadn't gone against Officer Shuno's orders, little Cera wouldn't be eating those berries right now."

"I know that, Troy," said Mr. Droma. "And we're grateful to you. But we can't go against Officer Shuno. He's the Second Commanding Officer. It's our job—our duty—to obey him."

"Even if it means letting your baby starve to death?"

Mr. Droma's face grew more tense. "Officer Shuno would never let that happen."

"What? Are you kidding me? Officer Shuno doesn't care what happens to your baby. Don't you realize that?"

Mr. and Mrs. Droma looked at each other, shocked.

"How can you say such a thing?" Mr. Droma cried incredulously. "You can't speak that way about him. Not only is it disrespectful, it's downright slanderous!" He looked at his wife, waiting for her to reply.

Mrs. Droma shook her head in disbelief. "That's a terrible thing to say! Besides, Chief Creta would never allow any harm to come to us."

Troy sighed, thoroughly disgusted. "Don't you people understand? Officer Shuno is insane. And I think he's holding Chief Creta prisoner in the town hall. Haven't you seen his armed guards strutting about? And do you really think Chief Creta would order something so stupid and senseless as having a new fence built around the old one? And what about the saltberries? Do you think Chief Creta would allow us to go for so many days without planting a new crop? Can't you see? Officer Shuno is behind all of this, and he doesn't care what happens to any of us!"

The Dromas were shocked.

"Now hold on there, Troy!" Mr. Droma said sternly, pointing a finger at him.

Troy had never before seen Mr. Droma so angry. But why? he wondered. I just saved his baby's life.

"My wife and I appreciate you coming over here and giving us your berries. We appreciate your concern. We can't thank you enough for what you've done. But I can't allow you to stand in my hut and talk that way about Officer Shuno. I'm afraid I'll have to ask you to leave."

Troy was stunned. "You ... you can't mean that. I just saved your baby's life! And now you're throwing me out?"

Mr. Droma hung his head. "I'm sorry, Troy," he said.

Troy glanced at Mrs. Droma, expecting her support. "Surely you don't feel that way, do you, Mrs. Droma?"

She quickly averted her eyes, looking down at Cera, who was now fast asleep in her arms. "I think you'd better go now, Troy," she said.

He felt his heart sink. "I can't believe what I'm hearing. I can't believe you mean it."

"I'm afraid we do mean it, Troy," said Mr. Droma. His voice was low, but tense. "My wife and I can't be—won't be—a party to that kind of talk. It's nothing personal." He went to the door, opened it. "It's just that ... well, you've got a lot to learn. You have to learn to respect your superiors. Officer Shuno is a good man. Chief Creta would've never put his faith in him if he wasn't worthy of it."

"But you don't underst—"

Mr. Droma held his hand up to cut him off. "It's *you* who doesn't understand, Troy. But you will. As you grow older, you'll come to realize that Officer Shuno *is* concerned about our welfare. That's his job—to lead us and protect us. You mustn't keep doubting him."

Troy met his eyes. "You're wrong, Mr. Droma. I only wish there was some way I could make you see how wrong you are—before it's too late." Mr. Droma frowned, nodded toward the open door.

Troy started to leave, then turned around. "I wish the best for you and your family, Mr. Droma. If you change your mind about helping me, you know where to find me. Just remember, though—Officer Shuno is mean and cunning. And he's got several henchmen who'll back him up. So if you decide to go up against him, keep a close eye on your wife and kids. It could become dangerous."

Mr. Droma shook his head sadly. "You haven't heard a word I said. Goodbye, Troy."

* * *

Early the next morning, Troy was awakened by loud knocking on his door. He jerked up in his straw cot, rubbing his eyes. But now that he was awake, the knocking had stopped. Must have been a dream, he thought.

Just then, someone began banging furiously on his door. "Open up in there!" a voice barked.

He scrambled out of bed, threw on his clothes, and raced to the door.

He had just barely lifted the two bolts when the door burst open, slamming against the wall. Sunlight flooded the room, momentarily blinding him.

Shocked, he threw his hands up against the glaring light, squinting through half-shut eyes. He was able to make out two bulky silhouettes standing in the doorway.

"Who are you? What do you want?" he cried, his heart hammering. The silhouettes came closer, until they were inside the hut.

Troy was horrified when he recognized Officer Shuno's guards. The taller one spoke first. "You have slandered Officer Shuno!" he barked. "Now, you must go to prison."

Before he could answer, they grabbed him by his arms and started toward the door. But a voice behind them stopped them. "What's going on here? What are you doing with my son?"

Troy's mom was standing in the hallway, bits of straw clinging to her mussed hair, her sleepy eyes squinting in the bright sunlight.

"We're taking him to the prison tree hut," the taller one answered. "Officer Shuno's orders."

"Officer Shuno's orders, my foot!" said Troy's mom, her face growing red with anger. "Leave my son alone, and get out of my house!"

"Yeah, sure, lady," the guard scoffed. He looked at the other guard and nodded toward the door.

As they started to leave again, Troy kicked his feet and thrashed his body, twisting against their hold. "Put me down!" he yelled.

He was no match against the two henchmen. They squeezed his arms so hard, he thought he would faint from the pain.

Troy thrust his head into the shorter guard's jaw. The guard cried out in pain, losing his grip on Troy.

At that moment, Troy's mom threw herself at the taller guard, gouging his eyes with her fingers.

The taller guard slammed Troy to the floor, then turned on his mom, backhanding her hard in the face.

She crumpled to the floor, unconscious.

The taller guard moved swiftly toward Troy, grabbed him by the top of his head, and yanked him to his feet. "Come on," he said to the shorter one, "let's get him locked up."

Resisting them with all his strength, Troy screamed, "Let me go! She's hurt! My mom is hurt! Let me go!"

They dragged him out the door and headed for the prison tree hut.

Chapter 9

The guards led Troy deep into the woods on a lesser path that branched off the main one. This old, abandoned trail was overgrown with weeds.

As the three of them rounded a bend, Troy was surprised to see Bree strolling towards them, carrying a pail of honey.

"Bree!" Troy cried, struggling against the guards' grasp.

Bree stopped abruptly. "Troy! What's going on?"

The taller guard spoke. "Well, well. Look who we have here."

Bree held the honey pail in front of her with both hands, nervously fingering the leather strap handle.

"We was just taking your little friend here to the prison tree hut," the shorter guard sneered, eyeing her from head to toe.

"Why?" she cried, her eyes meeting Troy's. "What's happened? What did you do?"

"I didn't do anyth—" Troy started to say, but was cut off abruptly by the taller guard.

"He's been going around saying bad things about Officer Shuno. Seems your boyfriend here don't like our Second Commanding Officer."

"Yeah," said the shorter one. "Now we gotta lock him up."

Bree's eyebrows lowered. "Lock him up? For how long?"

The two guards glanced at one another, grinning devilishly.

"We're just gonna throw away the key," the taller one said. "You may as well go and find yourself another boyfriend."

"You like short men?" the shorter guard asked.

The guards laughed fitfully.

Troy tried to squirm loose of their grasp. But it was no use, their grip was too strong. "Bree, listen carefully," he yelled. "My mom has been hurt. She's at home and she needs help. I need you to go over to Dr. Hadro's place and bring him back to my tree hut."

"Troy, don't worry. I'll go straight to Dr. Hadro's now, and later I'll talk to my dad about this prison business. Perhaps he can help you. Anyhow, I'll be by the prison later today to see you. Don't worry about your mom. I'll take care of it right away."

The guards, apparently astonished by her self-confidence, said nothing as she brushed past them.

"Thanks, Bree," Troy called after her as she disappeared around a bend.

"Should we go after her?" the shorter guard asked.

"Naw," the taller one replied. "Forget it. We got business to take care of with this one here." He thrust his hand into the back of Troy's head and clutched a handful of hair, shaking it gruffly.

Troy winced with pain, cursing the henchmen under his breath.

* * *

The prison tree hut was a dreary-looking place, built high in the upper branches of two tall trees. Their woody branches flared outward in a wide canopy over the large, round prison.

The entire structure—the floor, the roof, the walls—was built of thick posts lashed together with leather straps.

Standing at the foot of the prison tree stairs, Troy looked up. A shiver ran up his spine, and he shuddered. He had passed this forbidding place many times while hiking through the woods, searching for honey trees. And each time, he had been in awe of it, though he wasn't sure why. Perhaps it was the sheer size of it. Perhaps it was the dismal feeling of solitude that crept over him each time he passed by, knowing that in there, other people had lived—no, existed—in days gone by.

He recalled the story surrounding the prison tree hut that Chief Creta had told him. Built many years ago, long before Troy was born, the prison had been used as a holding tank for scores of villagers who had become drunk and disorderly after having guzzled ghastly amounts of saltberry wine. Most of the prisoners were released after having slept it off for a day or two. But some had remained for days on end, clinging to the safety of their cells, afraid to face the real world again.

But all of that was a thing of the past. Now-a-days, saltberry wine was illegal. It was against the law for anyone to make it, store it, sell it, or drink it. The wine had been the cause of too many fights on Spinosaur Island. And production of the life-sustaining saltberry crop had taken a severe plunge, for many of the workers could not show up for work after a nightlong drinking binge. Thus, Chief Creta had taken a vote among the islanders at the town square, and the majority of them had voted to outlaw the troublesome drink once and for all.

Since then, the prison had no longer been needed. It had been deserted for many years.

With the two guards following right behind him, Troy

started the long climb up the spiralling stairs. When they reached the top, they were met by two other guards who pushed Troy inside.

He found himself standing in a narrow, windowless corridor. Flaming torches sat high up in wooden brackets, flickering softly, casting deep shadows along the hallway.

The guard shoved him. "Come on, get moving. There's someone waiting to meet you."

Troy shuffled along, his feet padding softly on the plank floor. About halfway down the hallway, another corridor intersected it. From this intersection, he could see prison cells lined up on both sides.

They continued down to the end of the hall. There, the guard opened a thick plank door, revealing a large office.

Troy saw four more guards sitting around a square table, joking and laughing, and drinking from wooden mugs. On the table was a leather gourd, its opening corked at the moment. This must be the guards' station, he thought. Is that wine they're drinking? I wonder if Chief Creta knows about this?

"This is Troy," the guard said, shoving him toward the henchmen. "He's our first prisoner. Officer Shuno wants him locked up because he's a little troublemaker. He's all yours, Steg. Make sure he gets a cup of water and a half of saltberry a day—no more. Officer Shuno's orders."

Steg raised his mug to his lips, took a long drink, then set the mug down on the table and wiped his mouth with the back of his hand. Raising an eyebrow, he said, "So you're Troy, eh? Troy the troublemaker, eh?"

The other guards snickered.

Steg reached across the table, grabbed the gourd, uncorked it, and began pouring a dark blue liquid into his mug. "Care for some wine, lad?" The guards snickered again.

Troy ignored the question. The thought of these hench-men breaking the law, drinking wine, and snickering while his mother lay at home injured and helpless, really ticked him off. He felt his blood pounding in his temples, and he fought to control his anger. He cleared his throat, his fists clenched. "I'm not a troublemaker," he told Steg. "There's been a misunderstanding. I just wanna go home and take care of my mom. She's hurt real bad—thanks to your goons."

Steg was on his feet in a flash. The back of his heavy hand sliced through the air, smacking Troy in the mouth. "My name is Steg, sonny, and I don't take no back talk from my prisoners, eh?"

The blow hurtled Troy backwards, knocking him down. He struggled to his feet, dazed. Feeling a wetness on his mouth, he drew an arm across his lips, wiping a trickle of blood.

Steg grinned, baring broken teeth. He placed a beefy hand on top of Troy's head and grabbed a fistful of hair. "Come along then, sonny. I'll show you to your room, eh?"

Wincing with pain, Troy gritted his teeth as he was yanked to his feet. Dazed and weakened, he was defenseless against Steg's powerful grip.

Steg pulled him into the corridor, which was wide and circular in shape.

The prison tree hut was built like a giant wheel. The cells were lined up along both sides of the corridor, each secured with a thick plank door and a heavy wooden bar across its width.

"This one's as good as any, eh?" Steg said. Still clutching Troy's hair, he used his free hand to lift the bar and wrench the door open. He pushed Troy inside, slamming the door behind him.

On the wall opposite the door was a small window, about

two feet square, crisscrossed with wooden bars. The only light came from the single window.

Beneath the window was a pile of straw. Troy sat in the pile, his back leaning against the wall, knees drawn up, glancing around the room. It was bare, except for the straw.

Troy could hear the heavy wooden bar scrape into place. Then ... silence.

* * *

For several days, Troy spent his time lying in the straw, sleeping, thinking, worrying, then sleeping some more. He thought about his mom and wondered if she was okay. Had Bree been able to get Dr. Hadro to go see her? And what about Bree? She had promised to come and visit him and she never showed. Was Officer Shuno forbidding him visitors? If only I could get out of here, he thought. There has to be a way. Some way to escape ...

His thoughts were interrupted by a commotion. Through his cell window, he could hear a crowd of people clapping and whistling.

What's going on? he wondered, scrambling up to the window. In the distance he could see the saltberry field and people cheering.

Officer Shuno stood on the storage tree stairs, holding a bullhorn made of rolled up bark. He raised his arms toward the crowd, as though he were going to embrace them all.

The villagers fell silent as he put the bullhorn to his lips and started to speak.

Troy strained to hear.

"My fellow citizens," Officer Shuno began, "today is one of the most important days in our island's history. It is indeed a shame that Chief Creta has taken ill and cannot be here to share this glorious day with us. However, he has asked me to send his thanks and his profound gratitude to each and every one of you who has worked so hard these last several days building the new fence."

I just bet Chief Creta is sick today, Troy thought.

"And now that the new fence is done, and we have a new crop of berries planted, I wish to personally thank each and every one of you for your loyalty and your hard work. I assure you that our new, double-thick fence is now Spinosaur-proof."

The crowd exploded with cheers.

Officer Shuno continued. "Never again will we have to worry about those savages invading our field and eating our saltberries. It was through my leadership and your loyalty that we have seen our village through this crisis. Together, we have survived. And now that this crisis has passed, I would like to propose a day-long feast tomorrow. An entire day of celebration!"

The crowd applauded.

Officer Shuno raised his hands, silencing them. "First, we'll harvest our crop in the morning. Then we'll take our food back to the town square where we'll dine and sing and dance like never before. We'll even take some wine out of storage and use it to celebrate with—just this once!"

The crowd roared with approval.

Take some wine out of storage, my foot! Troy thought. No doubt Officer Shuno and his henchmen have been secretly making it and drinking it right along.

There was a noise outside the cell door—voices—barely audible. Then the scrape of the bar being lifted out of place. The door swung open.

Steg stepped in. "Eh, sonny. You got a visitor, eh? Heh, heh, heh," He looked toward the hallway and nodded.

Bree came in.

Troy threw his arms around her, buried his face in her hair. "Bree! Bree, I—" His voice choked off.

"Troy! Oh, Troy!" she said, holding him close. "I've missed you so!"

"Aaw ... now ain't that cute, eh?" Steg said sarcastically.

Troy had momentarily forgotten about Steg still standing there. He jumped to attention. "I ... ah ... "

Steg grinned, exposing his rotten and broken teeth. "Nice ... eh, sonny? Heh, heh, heh." He turned and swung the door shut behind him, sliding the bar into place.

Troy turned back to Bree, started to speak, but Bree stopped him with her kiss.

"I missed you, mister!" she blurted, gazing into his eyes. "I tried to get here sooner, but my parents ... well, you know."

"Yeah, I know. But its okay, Bree. I understand. I'm just so glad to see you." He hugged her again. Then, "How's my mom? Did you ever get a hold of Dr. Hadro?"

Bree's face lit up. "Oh, she's fine! Dr. Hadro came over right away and took care of her. He's been looking in on her every day, and he has a nurse staying with her day and night. And I've been getting over there most mornings, just to say hello and give Panga his treats." She smiled. "I think Panga and your mom *both* like me."

Troy felt relieved. "That's good to know. Thanks for your help, Bree."

"Don't mention it," she said smiling. "Oh, I almost forgot." She raised her right leg and crossed it over her left knee, her right heel turned upward. "I scraped off some pail-putty from one of my pails, and then I searched around and found *this*," she said, peeling something off the bottom of her foot. She held up a piece of flint, about two inches long and one inch wide.

Surprised, he took it from her and turned it over in his hands. Pressed on the back side of the stone blade was a small, flattened wad of his homemade putty. His face lit up.

"You're really something," he said, running his finger along the beveled edge of the blade. "This thing is sharp ... sharp enough to cut through leather thongs." He glanced at the lashings on the window bars.

She chuckled. "Well, that's the general idea. I figured they'd frisk me when I came to visit you. And I knew you'd be dying to get out of here. So I figured I'd smuggle it in on the bottom of my foot. "It was worth a try."

"You bet it was."

"I was praying that your putty was sticky enough to hold the flint in place until I reached you."

Still admiring the blade, Troy said, "Just think, this little tool is all I need to get out of here. It's my key to freedom." He looked at her, amazed. "You really are something else, you know that?"

"You're right," she said, smiling. "And so are you." She pecked him on the mouth.

He held up the flint. "I better hide this now." He went to the pile of straw and slipped it under, next to the wall. "It'll be safe here." He sat on the straw directly above the flint, leaning his back against the wall. "Come and sit down a while," he said, patting the straw next to him.

She went over and sat down next to him, leaning her head on his shoulder. "Do you know why you're here in the first place?"

"Well, they said I slandered Officer Shuno."

"Yeah, that's what I heard, too."

His face became sober. "It was the Dromas, wasn't it?"

She held his hand in hers. "Yes, it was. Mr. Droma went to the field the day after you saved his baby. He was explaining to everyone how you came over and gave your berries to them, saving little Cera's life. But then he started talking about the way you were running down Officer Shuno.

And then he bragged about how he asked you to leave, practically kicked you out of his hut. Unfortunately, a couple of Officer Shuno's henchmen overheard Mr. Droma. I guess they ran and told Officer Shuno about it. Needless to say, he got pretty sore about it."

"And that's why I'm here," said Troy.

"Right."

Troy shook his head. "I can't believe Mr. Droma would squeal on me like that. I mean, after I helped him with his baby and everything, you'd think he'd be at least a *little* loyal to me."

"He's a worm. What kind of person runs and tattles on someone after that someone saves his baby's life? That's the thanks you get for helping him out. In a way, you'd of been better off minding your own business and never going over there. At least then you wouldn't be in prison."

Troy was shocked. "Don't say that, Bree. If I didn't go over there, his little girl would have starved. It was the right thing—the only thing to do at the time. And I'm glad I was able to help little Cera."

Bree gazed at him, saying nothing. Then she stared down at the floor. Finally she smiled. She pecked him on his cheek. "That's why I love you."

He smiled. "I love you, too."

"So did you hear about the fence being done?" she asked.

"Yeah ... I heard."

"My parents are down there right now, listening to Officer Shuno's speech. We were there together, but I was able to ditch them in the crowd. That's how I was finally able to sneak up here and see you."

"I'm surprised Steg let you in."

"Oh, please! Don't even mention his name. Is he the grossest-looking thing, or what?"

Troy chuckled. "Well, he's not very pretty, is he?"

Her face took on a new seriousness. "Can you imagine what his wife must look like?"

Troy looked hard at her, his face grave. "He doesn't have a wife anymore." His tone was somber.

She looked at him, surprised. "What happened to her?"

"He had her for breakfast."

"Oh, you ..." she said, nudging him. Then she started giggling. And her giggling touched off his giggling. And his giggling ignited a new round of her giggling ... and on and on.

When they stopped to catch their breath, Troy thought about the new fence. "You know it won't work."

"What?"

"The new fence."

She hesitated, then said, "But I heard them say the double-thick fence is plenty thick enough to stop a Spinosaur."

Troy was exasperated. "I'm telling you that new fence is not Spinosaur-proof. Until someone rolls a boulder in front of the spot where they had chewed the hole, they'll come back night after night, gnawing their way in, eating our saltberries. I can't understand why I can't get anyone to believe me."

"I believe you, Troy," she said, patting his hand. "If you say the new fence won't work, then that's good enough for me. But don't expect the others to believe you. Officer Shuno and his guards have got everyone believing that you're a traitor."

"What? What's he talking about—a traitor?"

"Well, he's been telling everyone that this whole mess was your fault to begin with, and then you wouldn't even help to build the new fence, to correct the problem that you supposedly caused in the first place."

"What?"

"Yeah, and now he's actually convinced everyone that this entire island is better off with you in prison. I'm afraid the only people concerned about you are me, Mante, your mom, and Dr. Hadro."

"Oh, great."

"Well, at least now you know who your real friends are."

"Yeah, well, I don't see Mante over here, visiting me."

"He wanted to come," Bree explained. "But he's afraid he'll get into trouble, and then he'd be a prisoner in here, too."

"Yeah, I know. I don't blame him. It is pretty frightening. I mean, one look at Steg would keep me away from this place ... for good!"

She giggled, then sobered. "You know, he really is concerned about you, though." She shuddered. "He told me about the Spinosaur attack."

"Yeah, that was a close one—too close for comfort!"

"He's beating his brains out, thinking of a way to help you escape," Bree went on. "He wants to talk to Chief Creta about the whole mess, but they won't let him anywhere near the town hall tree hut. Come to think of it, they won't let *anyone* near there. It's so ... hush-hush. You know ... it's so mysterious and everything."

"Yeah, I know. I don't believe for a moment that Chief Creta is really sick. I think Officer Shuno may be holding him as a prisoner or something."

"Or worse," said Bree.

"Yeah ... or worse. I couldn't bare the thought of something bad happening to the Chief. He's been real good to me and my mom since my dad was killed. He's been like a grandfather to me—taught me a lot of stuff."

"He is such a kind and gentle person," Bree said, pondering. "Do you think Officer Shuno would really hurt him?"

"In a heartbeat," Troy answered. "He tried to kill me, didn't he?"

Bree shuddered again. "First the Troodon in your cupboard, then the rigged stairs." She slid her arms around his waist, held him close. "If you do escape, where will you go? What will you do?"

His face puckered. "I don't know. I can't go home. Officer Shuno's guards would look there first."

"Yeah," said Bree, "and then they'd probably check my place next."

"But I've been doing a lot of thinking in here about another idea I have," Troy went on, "concerning the castor-oil plant. I think I know how to—"

The sound of the heavy bar scraping startled him.

The door opened, and Steg poked his head in. "Hey, lass! Heh, heh, heh. Visiting hours are over, eh?"

Troy scrambled to his feet, extended his hand to Bree, then pulled her up. He slipped his arms around her and hugged her tight. "Take care," he whispered. "I love you."

"I love you, too," she squeaked. She tried to force a smile. "Bye," she said, her voice almost a whisper.

Troy bit his lip, trying hard to contain his tears as he watched her step into the hall.

"Aaw ... now ain't that touching, eh?" Steg said, then left the room, banging the door closed behind him.

Troy pounced on the pile of straw, then snatched the piece of flint. At the window, he began carving the leather thongs.

Chapter 10

Troy had been working on the leather lashing for only a few minutes when he heard a noise at the door. Someone was coming in. Frantically he buried the flint blade beneath the straw, then sat down on top of it.

Steg barged into the room. "I got me a feeling, eh?" he said, swaggering over to the window.

Troy's heart hammered, but he stretched his arms above his head and yawned, trying to conceal his terror. "Now what's the matter?" he asked, trying to sound unconcerned.

Steg grasped the oak bars on the window and gave them a tug. Instantly one of the thongs that Troy had been cutting popped free from the bars and fell on the floor. "Just as I thought, eh?" He turned to face Troy. "I don't know how she did it, eh? But she did it! Let's have it, then, eh?" he said, holding out his hand.

"Have what?" Troy said. "I don't have anyth—"

Steg grabbed him by the hair on top of his head and yanked him to his feet. "Now, sonny. I want it now, eh?" He slammed Troy into the wall, and Troy shrieked as pain shot through his body.

"Okay. I'll get it. I'll get it," he pleaded. He went to the straw, retrieved the flint, and handed it to Steg.

Steg grinned. "She's a clever one, eh?" he said, inspecting the blade. "Too bad she has to go to prison now, eh?"

"What for?" Troy asked, a feeling of doom beginning to spread over him.

"For trying to help you escape, eh?" He turned the blade over and over, examining it. "Real clever."

"But she doesn't have anything to do with it!" Troy cried. "I found it in my cell. She doesn't know anything about it."

Steg raised his thick, hairy eyebrows, looking Troy in the eye. "You think old Steg is dumb, eh? You'll learn, sonny. eh? Now come with me. We got to find you a new cell, eh?"

Troy eyed him with suspicion. "What for?"

"We can't let you stay in here, eh? Now that you've cut the bars on your window, eh?" He grabbed Troy's arm and led him into an identical cell next door.

Troy plopped himself down in the pile of straw.

"Take a good look around you, sonny. From now on, you get no food, no water, and no visitors. This here room is where you'll die, heh? Heh, heh, heh."

"I tried to escape, so now I have to die?" Troy asked incredulously. "That doesn't make any sense. You don't kill somebody for something like that." His face puckered. "You're not supposed to kill somebody for any reason. Not on *this* island. That's the law!"

"Heh, heh, heh. That was before Officer Shuno took over, eh? I expect things will be mighty different around here now, eh? Heh, heh, heh."

"Since when is Officer Shuno taking over? What happened to Chief Creta?"

"Oh, he's very sick, eh? He ain't gonna live but for a few more days, eh? Heh, heh, heh. Then Officer Shuno will be in charge."

Troy couldn't believe what he was hearing. So what am I supposed to do, he thought, sit around and let them kill the Chief?

He bit his lip. Over my dead body, he thought.

Steg lumbered over to Troy, grinning grotesquely. "They're gonna make me the new Second Commanding Officer. What da ya think of that, eh?"

"Congratulations," Troy said sarcastically.

"I'll drink to that! Heh, heh, heh."

* * *

It was early morning when Troy was awakened by a loud noise reverberating throughout the forest.

The horn, Troy thought, scrambling out of the straw. Someone's blowing the horn in the town square. Something's happened.

He looked out the window at the saltberry field far away. He was shocked, but not surprised, at what he saw.

A crowd of villagers was gathered in front of the gate. Clearly, they were in a state of panic. Before them lay a huge hole in the fence in the exact same spot as before. Apparently the Spinosaurs had chewed through *both* layers of fencing—the new and the old. The field was littered with Spinosaur tracks.

The saltberries were gone.

Troy could not control himself. He started screaming out the window.

"YOU FOOLS! I WARNED YOU! BUT YOU WOULDN'T LISTEN TO ME! YOU WOULDN'T BELIEVE ME! NOW MAYBE YOU'LL STAND UP TO OFFICER SHUNO AND PUT A STOP TO THIS MADNESS!"

His throat ached, and he knew the people couldn't hear him, being so far away. But he had to do *something*, otherwise he would've burst from sheer frustration.

He was startled by the sound of the wooden bar being

knocked out. The heavy door burst open and Steg charged into the room.

"Wha da ya think you're doing, yelling out the window like that, eh? Who do ya think you are, eh? Still slandering Officer Shuno?" His fists hovered dangerously close to Troy's face.

Troy's heart raced. "I-I-I—"

Steg fired a kick into Troy's shin, making him cry out in pain.

"Maybe I oughta just finish you off, eh?" Steg said, shaking a fist in Troy's face. "Why waste time starving you to death, eh?"

Troy threw his hands up to protect himself, waiting for the assault. But nothing happened. The attack never came.

Suddenly Steg's face softened—a little—and his fists uncurled. "What am I gonna do with ya, eh? You're just a kid." He sighed, shaking his head. "Just a kid, eh? Too bad." He turned and started to leave.

Seeing an opening, Troy spoke. "Wait!" he pleaded. His leg throbbed from Steg's kick. "Don't leave yet. Please!"

"What is it, then? Eh? I ain't got all day, ya know."

"What is Officer Shuno going to do about the Spinosaurs and the hole in the fence? And what about the saltberry crop? It's been days now since any berries have been harvested. Our people are tired and hungry. They can't live on honey forever. How much more can they take?"

"Hah! Don't you be worrying about that now," Steg said, smirking. "Officer Shuno knows just what to do. He'll show them beasts who's the boss, eh?"

Troy rolled his eyes impatiently. "Unless you roll a boulder in front of the hole, the Spinosaurs will continue to show *you* who's the boss."

Steg took a menacing step forward, his face scowling.

Troy held his hands up in front of his face, defending himself. "Take it easy!" he blurted. "I'm just worried about our people, that's all. What will they eat? How will they survive? And how are they gonna stop the Spinosaurs?"

"Hah! We don't have to starve you to death, eh? You'll kill yourself from worrying so much, eh? Heh, heh, heh. I told you, Officer Shuno has everything under control, eh?"

"But how?"

Steg raised an eyebrow. "How, eh? I'll tell you how. At this very moment, he's at the town square telling everyone to make torches and dip 'em in tallow, eh?"

"What for?"

"What for, eh? To keep them beasts away from our berries tonight, that's what for!" He smiled confidently, his huge hands on his hips. "I told you we have everything under control, eh, sonny? Heh, heh, heh."

Troy's mouth dropped open. "You've got to be kidding!" he cried. "It'll never work! Our people could get killed!"

Steg threw his head back and laughed. "Hah! It'll work all right, eh? You wait ... you'll see."

Troy lowered his head, shaking it disbelievingly. He took a deep breath, forced a smile, and said, "Look ... it's too dangerous. Can't you see that? What do you think's gonna happen when the torches burn out?"

"Hah! What do ya think, eh? We'll have hundreds of people down there, guarding the field, re-dipping their torches whenever they have to, eh? We'll keep 'em lit all night. That'll keep them beasts away, eh? Heh, heh, heh."

Troy felt his mouth going dry, his heart beating faster. I can't believe these guys are so ignorant, he thought. "What about the next night? And the night after that? And the night after that? There isn't enough tallow on this island to keep all those torches burning night after night, forever. I'm telling you, our people will die out there." He kicked at a tuft of straw on the floor. "Another great idea by the great Officer Shuno."

Steg's heavy hand smacked Troy's mouth. The blow sent him sprawling backwards. The last thing he heard before he blacked out was Steg's deep, gruff voice. "I'll not put up with the likes of you, eh?"

* * *

When Troy woke up in his cell, it was dark. Wind whistled through the bars on the window, and with it came the unmistakable smell of smoke. He rolled over on his back, yawning. Pain stabbed his jaw where Steg had hit him. He ran his fingers over his swollen lips.

Chilly in here, he thought, snuggling deeper in the straw, his eyes still closed. Still smell smoke. Can't be. Must be dreaming.

Suddenly the night was shattered by a distant bloodcurdling scream. Troy jerked awake, his heart pounding.

He jumped to his feet, glanced out the window, then froze with shock when he saw what was happening.

"The torches!" he cried. "The wind! How could they be so stupid!"

The section of fence where the hole had been patched was ablaze. The flames roared upward, licking viciously at the night sky. Everything was bathed in a red-orange glow. Huge balls of fire sprang from the fence, toward the forest, threatening to set it ablaze as well.

Several people were on fire and were frantically running about, screaming and slapping themselves. But their efforts to extinguish themselves was in vain, and Troy watched in horror as one by one they dropped dead in the field.

One flaming man bolted through the gate toward the forest, screaming for his life, a pack of Spinosaurs close behind him. The beasts were on him in an instant, and his screaming stopped abruptly.

Spinosaurs surrounded the saltberry field, many of them finding their way inside through the open gate, keeping their distance from the section of flaming fence. Some of them chased the screaming people, forcing many to find refuge in the storage tree hut. Other Spinosaurs were drawn to the saltberries that dotted the field, and hungrily devoured them one by one, temporarily ignoring the frenzy of fleeing people.

Amazingly, dozens of men had already run to the lake with empty pails to fetch water, and were now returning with the first of the bucket brigade. It was hazardous work as the fire was being extinguished, the flames getting smaller and smaller, and the Spinosaurs venturing closer and closer.

Some of the men were picked off by Spinosaurs as they made a desperate attempt to return to the lake for more water. Their screams could be heard above the other peoples' yelling, the Spinosaurs' roaring, and the violent wind blowing. Just as the flames appeared to be under control, another gust of wind would fan the flames, igniting a new inferno.

"This is insane!" Troy yelled. He threw himself against his cell door, pounding it, kicking it. "Let me out of here, you maniacs! Let me out!"

He heard the bar sliding out of place. As the door opened, candlelight flooded the room, and Steg stuck his face in.

"I'll not stand for your nonsense anymore, sonny," he growled.

The candle flame wavered for an instant in the draft, then blew out.

"Eh?"

Instantly, Troy launched himself past Steg, then raced down the torch-lit corridors.

"Come back here!" Steg barked.

Troy could hear his heavy footsteps, but he was way ahead of him. "I'm out of here!" he yelled.

As he approached the prison exit, he saw two guards standing with their backs toward him, blocking his path. One was armed with a bow, and a leather quiver filled with arrows hung from his shoulder. The other was armed with a spear.

I won't give them time to use their weapons, he thought, racing toward them.

Before they could turn and look his way, he burst through the doorway, knocking them off balance. He took the stairs two at a time, descending quickly into the darkness.

Behind him a voice shouted, "Stop him! Don't let him escape!" Then he heard heavy footsteps on the stairs.

As he scrambled, sudden pain ripped into his leg. It was pain he had never known. Instantly he stumbled and fell headfirst, tumbling down several steps before crashing into the railing.

"I'm hit!" he shrieked, clutching an arrow protruding from his left calf.

In the darkness he heard footsteps coming down the stairs toward him. Then he heard the guards' voices, and he was illuminated by their torchlight as they got closer.

Standing over him, one of them said, "I guess I'm a better bowman than I thought."

"Yeah," said the other. "Not everyone can hit a moving target in the dark."

"Just luck," replied the bowman. Then they both laughed.

Far below in the saltberry field, a new wave of screaming and yelling erupted. Spinosaurs growled and squealed. The guards kept laughing.

Troy heard more footsteps coming down the stairs. He

looked up and saw Steg approaching, his scowling face looming in the torchlight.

"You got him, eh? Nice shot, eh? Good for you, man," Steg said, patting the bowman on his back. "Good for you!"

"I'm hurt!" Troy cried, holding his leg. "Help me!"

"Hah!" said Steg. "You'll get no help from us, eh? You're more trouble than you're worth, eh?" He turned to the bowman and said, "Finish him!"

The bowman strung an arrow on his bow, stretching the string back in a wide arch, aiming at Troy's chest.

Troy's eyes grew wide with fear, his entire body turning liquid. He threw his hands up for protection, anticipating the razor sharp tip of the flint arrowhead to pierce his chest at any moment.

Just then, a commotion of footsteps and voices erupted from below. Troy turned his head and saw faces and torches rounding the tree trunk on the spiral stairs. People were approaching. Officer Shuno's voice called out from the darkness. "Stop! Don't be a fool!" He stepped forward, clutching a torch. "I told you—it has to look like an accident!"

More faces and torches drew nearer. Standing behind Officer Shuno was Bree, framed between two other guards.

"Bree!" Troy cried.

She rushed to him, knelt beside him. "Troy! What have they done to you?" She gasped when she saw the arrow jutting out of his leg. She looked up at Steg and the bowman. "You filthy creeps! Look what you've done!" she screamed, tears rolling down her cheeks.

"Bree, don't," Troy gasped, gritting his teeth against the pain.

Officer Shuno's face began shaking, his eyes bulging with madness. "Enough!" he exploded. "Take them away and lock them up! No food. No water. No visitors. Ever!"

Steg rubbed his grizzly chin. "Boss? What about the arrow, eh?"

Officer Shuno glared at him. "What about it?"

"Want me to remove it, eh?"

Officer Shuno looked down at Troy. Their eyes met and locked in the torchlight. An evil grin slowly spread across his face. "Why bother?"

"What about her, eh?" Steg asked, pointing at Bree. "She gets her own cell, eh?"

"No! Lock them up together," Officer Shuno snapped. "I want them to watch each other starve to death!" He turned and started to descend the stairs.

"Wait!" Troy cried, wincing with pain, blood dripping from his wound.

Officer Shuno stopped and turned around, his face harsh and pinched. "Please help the others," Troy pleaded. "They're getting killed down there!"

"THEN LET THEM DIE!" Officer Shuno roared, his voice booming, drowning out the chaos below.

* * *

Alone in their cell, Troy and Bree huddled together on the straw. Light from the towering flames streamed through the window.

His leg was growing numb.

"We have to remove the arrow," he said, lying on his back. "Hurry up, we're losing time."

She looked at him, puzzled. "What are you talking about?"

"We gotta save Chief Creta. We're getting out of here—right now."

"How?"

He smiled. "Don't worry, I've got it all figured out. First we—"

"What's to figure out?" she interrupted. "First they throw

you in prison for slandering Officer Shuno. Then, tonight, they come by my hut to take me to prison for giving you the flint blade. My father doesn't even know yet that I'm here. He's still down at the field with the others, fighting the Spinosaurs and trying to put out the fire. My mother's a basket case, fit to be tied. So what's left to figure out?" She crossed her arms over her chest, frowning. "We're not going *anywhere.*"

Troy was growing impatient. "Like I said, we're getting out of here right now. We're gonna save ourselves and we're gonna save Chief Creta."

"But how?"

"Pull the arrow out. Then use the arrowhead to cut the thongs on the window bars. Then tie one of the thongs around my leg, above the wound, to stop the bleeding." He paused.

She stared at him, waiting. "And then?"

"And then ... I hope you're a good tree climber."

Her mouth dropped open and her eyes widened in amazement. "You're incredible!" she said. Then her face sobered and she gazed at him. "I always could count on you, mister."

He kissed her gently, then said, "Come on—there's no time to lose."

She grasped the arrow with both hands. "Hang on. Here it goes." She began pulling.

Gritting his teeth against the pain, he stifled a scream when the arrow came out. Sitting up with his back against the wall, he planted his fingers over the wound and pressed down hard, slowing the flow of blood.

Bree scrambled to the window with the sharp arrowhead and cut the thongs off the bars. Then she tied one on his leg above the wound, fashioning a crude tourniquet.

The bleeding stopped.

"Time to go save the Chief," he said, rising to his feet.

But as he stood up, a wave of dizziness swept over him. He stumbled into the wall, then hooked his arms over the sill. Throbbing pain ripped through his leg.

"That does it, Troy. You're too weak. We're not going anywhere tonight. We'll have to wait until tomorrow night, when you're stronger. Meanwhile, I'll wedge the bars back into place—just in case."

"No!" he gasped, straightening up. "The longer we wait, the more people will die out there. It's up to us. We gotta save the Chief. It's now or never."

"But, you're hurt," she cried.

"I'll make it," he said. "Come on ... we can do this. Just follow me. And don't make a sound."

They slipped quietly through the window, and out into the darkness.

Chapter 11

Troy led the way through the twisted mass of gnarled branches. He paused often, looking back over his shoulder, making sure Bree was keeping up with him. Carefully, he began inching his way down. When he was almost there, he stopped and waited, listening for sounds of any guards that may be lurking on the ground beneath them.

Below, at the saltberry field, flames still raged, people screamed, and Spinosaurs squealed and roared.

As he sat waiting in a branch above the spiral stairs, Bree crawled along the limb, then straddled it, sitting next to him.

"Think it's safe to go down?" she whispered.

"I don't know."

"Can you see any guards?"

Straining, he peered through the branches below, searching for any movement or shadowy figures. But aside from the glow of the fire, everything was black. He wouldn't be able to see any guards unless he practically bumped into them.

"I don't know. I can't see." he whispered.

"How's your leg?"

"It's swollen, but it's not bleeding."

"Does it hurt?"

"Just a little," he lied. By now his leg felt as if it were on fire, and the pain was slowly spreading up his calf and into his thigh.

"Can you make it?"

"I have to."

"No, you don't. We could go back. Wait until tomorrow, when you're stronger."

"No way. Tomorrow's too late."

A gust of wind rocked the tree, blasting its branches, threatening to knock them off their perch.

"Hold on," he whispered loudly above the wind. Then he lay flat on his stomach, pressing his cheek into the knotty branch, his arms wrapped tightly around it. The wind was relentless, blasting again and again. Each gust forced smoke into his eyes and nose.

"Let's go down," he called over his shoulder.

"I'm right behind you," she called back.

He jumped down onto the stairs, and Bree followed. Leading her by the hand, he crept to the bottom of the prison tree. At ground level, he stood for a few moments, catching his breath. "We're gonna make a beeline for the seashore, where panga's sleeping. We'll need his help to save the Chief. Hold on to my hand and don't let go. When we get on the path, just keep running. Don't stop—no matter what."

Bree pointed toward the saltberry field. "Troy, look!"

Troy gaped at the fiasco. It appeared that the fire was being confined to that portion of fence where the hole had been and the gated area, thanks to the efforts of dozens of men who were gallantly dousing the flames with buckets of water, while dodging marauding Spinosaurs. Hundreds of people were still trapped inside the fence, along with dozens of Spinosaurs. Their pathetic screams could be heard above the wind, reaching far into the night.

"My dad's out there," she said, her voice cracking.

He embraced her. "I'm sorry, Bree. But there's nothing we can do now. Our only hope is to save the Chief. Only he can put a stop to Officer Shuno's madness."

She stared at him through tears. "But how?"

"Come on. I'll show you."

As they raced through the moonlit forest, Troy was certain they would encounter one or more Spinosaurs along the way. But they hadn't. They must all be at the saltberry field, he thought, eating saltberries—and people. He shuddered at the thought.

Now, as Troy and Bree approached the shoreline, he could see the heads and long necks of several Saltasaurs silhouetted against the moonlit sky, their bodies safely submerged beneath the ocean, just a few yards from the shore.

Walking out across the sand, toward the water, Troy cupped his hands around his mouth and called to Panga. "Panga! Here, boy! Panga!"

Suddenly one of the silhouettes swiveled its head and blasted air through its nostrils, making a snorting sound. Then it slowly moved through the water, toward Troy.

Panga lumbered out of the water and up onto the shore.

Troy patted the dinosaur's humongous front leg. "Good boy, Panga. "Let's go for a ride."

Panga lowered his head until it was only two feet above the ground. "Hop on," Troy said.

Bree and Troy straddled the long, muscular neck.

As Panga raised his head high into the air, Bree asked, "Is this safe?"

"Yeah," said Troy. "Just hold on tight." Then he tapped Panga's neck with his foot and said, "Let's go, boy. It's time to save Chief Creta."

* * *

As they approached the town hall tree, Troy saw two guards on the town hall platform, blocking the stairs to Chief Creta's hut, the tips of their spears glinting in the moonlight.

Clinging high up on Panga's neck, Troy steered the Saltasaur toward the opposite side of the tree, keeping them out of sight. Moonlight dappled the forest, and the wind howled ferociously, mercifully masking any noise they might have made as they approached, hidden in the brush. When Panga's head was level with the window to Chief Creta's hut, Troy and Bree slipped off of his neck and into the darkened room.

"Stay here, boy," Troy told Panga.

The tame Saltasaur obeyed the command and stood right outside the window, waiting.

Troy stepped to one side of the window and pulled Bree alongside him. "Shhh," he told her. Had anyone heard them come in? he wondered. He held his breath, listening.

At first, dead silence.

But a moment later, he heard muffled voices and recognized one of them as Officer Shuno's.

Troy's eyes were not yet used to the darker inside. On the opposite wall, a slit of candlelight squeezed beneath a door.

Bree stirred beside him. "They'll kill us if they find us in here," she whispered.

"Shhh."

She whispered, "The Chief's probably in there with them. Now we'll never be able to save him."

"Shhh."

Just then, Troy heard a quiet moan in the darkness.

"Shhh." He felt Bree stiffen next to him. His heart raced. The moan had been faint, very faint. But he had heard it nonetheless. Or had he?

As he started to move away from the thatched wall, he heard the moaning again, louder this time. His heart nearly stopped, then raced with fury.

Bree tightened her grip on his hand.

Another moan.

Then, more voices and laughter in the next room.

Sounds like they're having a damn party in there, Troy thought. Our people are dying down at the field, and those creeps are in there, celebrating!

Another moan.

Troy's eyes finally adjusted to the darkness, and he found himself staring at a cot against the far wall. The longer he stared, the more the shadows seemed to melt away, and he became aware of a figure lying on the straw cot.

He whispered to Bree, "Whoever it is, he doesn't seem to be aware of us."

She put her lips to his ear. "Who could it be?"

Suddenly it dawned on him.

Could it be? Was it him? Chief Creta? With Bree at his side, he crept up to the cot. Even in the darkness, he could see the sunken eyes and the hollowed cheeks. A leather strap stretched across the mouth.

"Chief Creta!" Troy whispered, kneeling beside the cot. Are you all right?" He reached behind the elderly man's head and untied the gag.

Bree put her hand on his forehead. She gasped when she saw the haggard face. "Oh, my God! Is he all right?" she whispered.

Chief Creta moaned and tried to speak.

"Shhh," said Troy. He put his hands on the Chief's face. "Chief Creta?" he whispered. "It's me—Troy."

The Chief's eyes fluttered and his lips trembled. "Water!" he sputtered. "Give me water."

"Now what'll we do?" Bree whispered. "He's dying of thirst!"

The Chief's eyes fluttered. "On the chair," he gasped. "Water pouch." His eyes dropped shut.

Troy found the leather pouch hanging from the chair. He tugged the cork out with his teeth, then held the gourd out to the Chief. "Here, Sir. Drink," he whispered.

But the Chief didn't move. He lay motionless, his eyes still closed. His breathing was hard and strained. "Water," he gasped. "Please ... give me water."

It was then Troy noticed the leather straps that bound the Chief's hands and feet. He practically choked on the lump that swelled in his throat. "How could anyone do this to you?" he whispered, blinking back tears. "Those dirty bastards!"

Never before in his life had Troy felt that degree of hate for anyone. But he felt it now, as he stared at the helpless old man before him; a man who had been like his grandfather; a man who had been so kind to him and his mom when his dad had been killed; a man who had always showed only kindness and caring toward his people; a man who Troy was now more determined than ever before to save; a man for whom Troy would gladly give his life for, if it came to that.

Chief Creta moaned again, his eyes fluttering.

Bree took the pouch from Troy. "Here," she whispered, "I'll give him water. You untie him." As she held the pouch to the Chief's lips, Troy untied the straps, then gingerly removed them.

As Chief Creta slurped the water, Troy wondered if he would ever again see the familiar twinkle in the old Chief's eyes. He looks so frail, so withered, so broken, he thought sadly. He needs food! Troy got up and went to a cupboard on the opposite wall. Inside he found two dried and shriveled saltberries and a bowl of honey.

When the Chief finished drinking, Bree fed him the berries and a few spoonfuls of honey. He ate slowly. When he finished, he sighed deeply and gazed up at Troy and Bree.

"Feeling better, Sir?" Troy whispered.

The Chief spoke softly. "Yes. Thank you." His lips trembled. "It's been days since I've eaten or drunk anything."

"Then it's true!" Troy blurted in a loud whisper. "They *are* trying to starve you to death!"

The Chief nodded.

"But, why?" Bree whispered.

Still lying on his back, Chief Creta drew a deep breath, then exhaled slowly. "The Second Commanding Officer would take my place. Becomes the new Chief. It's the law of our land." He hesitated, catching his breath, then went on. "Apparently Officer Shuno can't wait to become the new Chief."

"But that's murder!" Troy whispered.

"Our people wouldn't stand for it," Bree whispered.

Chief Creta asked for more water, took a drink, then wiped his mouth. "They wouldn't know it was murder," he said, his voice low and scratchy. "Officer Shuno plans to tell everyone that I died of an illness due to old age. Because I would've died by starvation, there wouldn't be any bruises, no wounds. No one would ever suspect murder."

In the next room, Officer Shuno and his henchmen could be heard talking loudly, joking and laughing.

"Do his guards know about this?" Troy whispered, horrified.

"Some of them do, but I'm not sure if they all do," Chief Creta said, his breath labored. "I don't even know how many guards he has."

"The place is crawling with them," Troy whispered.

Bree whispered, "He probably keeps half of them here, and the other half at the prison tree hut."

The Chief's face puckered. "Why the prison tree hut? It's been closed down for years."

"Not anymore it isn't," Troy whispered. He explained to the Chief what had happened on the island since the Chief was kidnapped. He told him how he and Bree had been taken prisoners. He told him how Officer Shuno had ordered everyone to build a new double-thick fence, and how it had caught fire and was burning this very minute.

"A maniac!" Chief Creta cried in his low, raspy voice. "He knows better than to have our people at the field after dark. Even with torches, they haven't got a chance against the Spinosaurs! It's insane!"

"That's not the worst of it," Troy whispered. "Apparently Officer Shuno expects our people to defend our saltberry crop against the Spinosaurs *every* night."

Chief Creta jerked up from the cot, propping himself on his elbows. "He must be stopped!" he cried. His voice was low and hoarse, but he spoke with intensity. "You *must* convince the others he's mad. Tell them I sent you. Tell them to stop fighting the Spinosaurs and get into the safety of their homes. They'll all be slaughtered. Tell them *I* command it."

"But I've tried to tell them, Sir," Troy whispered. "That's why I came here several days ago with Bree and Mante. I was trying to convince them that something was wrong, that you were in danger. But then you came to the door and told us that we should follow Officer Shuno's orders.

The Chief rested his head back on the cot. "I'm sorry I did that, but I had no choice. Officer Shuno was holding a spear in my back. If I had yelled for help and alerted you, his guards would have killed all three of you on the spot."

"We understand," Bree whispered. "But I don't think anyone will ever listen to us now. You'll have to tell them yourself."

"But how?"

"My pet Saltasaur, Panga, is waiting right outside your window," Troy whispered. "We're taking you out of here, to-night!"

"But I can't," the Chief protested. "I'm too—"

A noise outside the door stopped him abruptly. A rumbling of voices grew louder in the next room. Troy grabbed Bree's shoulders and forced her down on the floor in front of the cot. "Stay here," he whispered. "Don't move!" He scampered around the cot and flattened himself against the wall next to the door.

The wooden door creaked open, spilling candlelight in the room.

"Ponte! What are you doing in there?" Officer Shuno's voice barked.

"You said you wanted some berries, Sir. I thought I'd use up the ones in Chief Creta's room first. *He* won't be needing them."

"There's nothing but *dried* berries in there. I specifically told you I wanted *fresh* saltberries. Now go and fetch them from *my* cupboard, you moron."

"Yes, Sir. Right away, Sir."

The door closed and once again the room was dark.

Troy listened intently, his heart pounding furiously. He waited a moment, then went to the Chief. "You ready to go?" he whispered.

The Chief nodded. "You'll have to carry me to the window."

Chapter 12

With Bree and Chief Creta riding on Panga's back, and Troy riding up high on Panga's neck, near his head, Troy was able to steer the beast in the moonlit darkness, through the forest, all the way to Dr. Hadro's tree hut. Not wanting to risk going through the window with the feeble Chief, Troy and Dr. Hadro carried him up the stairs to Dr. Hadro's office.

"Put him on the cot, and let's have a look at him," Dr. Hadro said, clearly upset at the old Chief's condition.

Later, after a thorough examination, Dr. Hadro offered Chief Creta more water, berries, and honey.

As the Chief sat, eating slowly and quietly, Troy asked, "Will he be okay, Doctor?"

"Yes," said Dr. Hadro. "He'll be fine. I expect a full recovery in just a few days. But if he had gone another day without food or water, he might very well have died within a day."

"It was that close?" asked Bree.

"It was that close," said Dr. Hadro. Then, to Troy he said, "I better take a look at that leg of yours. I noticed you were limping on it before. What happened?"

"He was shot by one of Officer Shuno's guards with a bow and arrow," Bree said.

Dr. Hadro shook his head in disgust, then pointed Troy to a chair, motioned for him to sit down. "Does it hurt?" he asked, examining the wound.

"A little," Troy lied again. Actually his leg thudded with pain.

"Hmmm," said Dr. Hadro, frowning. "This will get infected if we don't clean it."

"Will he be all right?" Bree asked, standing behind Troy, her hands on his shoulders.

"Sure, sure," said Dr. Hadro. "Not to worry. I'll have him fixed up in no time."

While Dr. Hadro cleaned the wound, Troy, Bree, and Chief Creta filled him in on Officer Shuno's plot for a takeover.

"There's nothing I can do tonight," said Dr. Hadro, standing over Troy's leg, stirring a blue liquid in a bowl. "But first thing tomorrow, I'll stop in and see your parents, let them know what's going on."

"How is my mom?" Troy asked, worried.

"She's doing fine, son. She had a concussion, and I had to put a few stitches in her scalp, but she's fine now." He spooned the blue liquid onto Troy's wound.

"Yeow!" Troy cried, his body stiffening.

"Sorry, son. I didn't mean to hurt you," said Dr. Hadro.

"What is that stuff?" Bree asked.

"It's fermented saltberry juice," the doctor replied. "It's an antiseptic. It kills germs."

"That reminds me," said Troy. "I think I've come up with an idea to stop the Spinosaurs from attacking our saltberry field once and for all."

Chief Creta leaned forward on the cot he was sitting on, his eyes alert. "Let's hear it, son."

"Well," Troy began, "I discovered that the castor-oil plant is very poisonous. It made Panga real ill when he ate some. I have a plan to extract a syrup from the plants, and paint it on the fence surrounding the saltberry field. I believe the painted surface would then become toxic, and kill or repel the Spinosaurs when they tried to chew on it."

Bree gasped, came around to the front of Troy's chair, bent over, and hugged him. "That's my man!" she cried, beaming.

"Well, I'll be ... " said Dr. Hadro, as he finished wrapping a burlap bandage around Troy's wound. "You know, that just might work!"

Chief Creta chuckled, coughed, then chuckled some more. Then, his face sober, he said, "If we get through this alive, lad, I'd be proud to have you as my new Second Commanding Officer."

"Thank you, Sir," Troy said. And now he was beaming—despite the immense burning pain in his leg.

"Well, I'm all done here," said Dr. Hadro, gathering up his medical supplies. "You keep an eye on that leg, make sure it doesn't get infected."

"Thanks, Doc," Troy said. "And thanks for helping my mom."

"You're quite welcome, son," said Dr. Hadro. "I was glad to help."

"Well, what do we do now?" Bree asked. "Where should we go?"

"You're welcome to stay here," said Dr. Hadro. "There's plenty of room."

"No," said Troy. "That won't work. If Officer Shuno or his guards discover we've escaped from prison, or that Chief Creta is no longer in his room, they may come looking for us here."

"Same thing with going to either of our houses," said Bree.

"Right," said Troy.

"Then where?" asked Dr. Hadro.

"The three of us will have to spend the night at the cave, down by the lake," said Troy. "Panga can take us there. We'll be safe inside the cave, the Spinosaurs can't reach us there. And Panga can spend the night in the deeper part of the lake, where the Spinosaurs won't be able to reach him, either."

"Excellent idea," said Chief Creta, who was now lying down on the cot.

"But are you up to it, Sir?" asked Bree, worried.

"Oh, you just get me back on that Saltasaur, and I'll take it from there. That was the best ride of my life!" said the Chief, already his wit and humor starting to return. But then his tone became serious. "Dr. Hadro?"

"Yes, Sir?" '

"Tomorrow morning I want you to not only notify these kids' parents and tell them what's been going on, but I also want you to round up as many of your trusted friends as you can find, and tell them about Officer Shuno's plan for a take-over. Then I want you to take them with you to the town square, where you'll use the horn and alert the entire village."

"Yes, Sir," said Dr. Hadro. "And then?"

"As soon as we hear that horn blow," said the Chief, "the three us will ride in on Panga, and meet you with the others at the town square. I'll personally speak to the villagers and set the record straight, let them know what's *really* been going on." He paused, then said, "It's time to take our island back!"

"Yes, Sir!" Dr. Hadro gushed, obviously elated. "It's time, indeed!"

* * *

Later, after the Chief had been safely loaded back onto Panga, with Troy and Bree accompanying him, the three of them were on their way to the lakeside cave. They carried with them a water gourd and a honey gourd, but no saltberries. Dr. Hadro's meager supply of berries had been completely used up during their visit. The entire village must be close to being out of berries as well, Troy thought. But tomorrow we'll plant another crop—no matter what.

His thoughts were interrupted by an ear-piercing squeal somewhere behind them in the moonlit forest. He felt Panga tense, then quicken his gait.

"My God, that sounds close!" Bree cried.

"It was close," Troy agreed. "Hold on tight—both of you. We're almost there."

Troy noticed the wind had completely stopped and the forest was now eerily still.

Too still. Not even a cricket could be heard.

Another high-pitched squeal.

Branches snapping.

Getting closer.

Panga's lumbering gait had now become a trot, his huge torso bouncing and swaying, crashing through underbrush, snapping branches like toothpicks.

With his arms and legs wrapped around Panga's neck, Troy clung for his life. Looking down over his shoulder at Bree and Chief Creta, he was terrified that they would lose their grip and slide off of Panga's back. When he looked up again, he saw it shimmering in the moonlight, dead ahead. The lake!

"Hold on!" Troy yelled over his shoulder. "We're almost there!"

Panga broke through the underbrush and plowed onto the sandy shore.

They were so close now, Troy could see the mouth of the cave, bathed in moonlight, beckoning him.

The noises behind them had stopped.

Almost there, Troy thought. Can't be more than a hundred feet. "We're gonna make it!" he cried. "Good boy, Pang—"

Suddenly a Spinosaur burst through the bushes flanking the cave directly in front of them. Unleashing an ear-shattering roar, the beast lunged for Panga.

Snorting out of fear, Panga stopped dead in his tracks then reared up on his hind legs, dumping Troy, Bree, and Chief Creta into the sand.

The Spinosaur's crocodile-like jaws snapped and popped, grazing Panga's chest.

Another thunderous roar shattered the nighttime quiet.

Panga came down on all fours in an obvious effort to stomp his attacker.

But he missed.

The Spinosaur squealed, then lunged at Panga again, knocking him to the ground with a mighty rumble. As the savage beast closed in, ready for the kill, it suddenly caught sight of Troy, Bree, and Chief Creta who were still sprawled in the sand, struggling to get up.

The beast stopped, cocked its enormous head, the bony tips of its spine-studded sail glinting in the moonlight. It stared at the three of them through slitted eyes glowing red in the dark. The creature lowered its head almost to the ground, sniffing loudly. It stopped abruptly and was suddenly rigid. Then it jerked erect, threw its head back, and roared, exposing rows of sharp teeth. Then it exploded with renewed ferocity and practically leaped in a single bound, hovering over the three of them.

Bree screamed with the intensity of a lightning strike. Troy tried to shield her and Chief Creta with his body, as futile as that may have been.

Just as he looked up, expecting to catch his last glimpse

of life, he heard a WHOOSH!-CRACK! and a huge, thick object whizzed overhead, a giant blur before his eyes. A split second later, the Spinosaur collapsed in a humongous heap on the beach, its great head and neck twisted grotesquely.

Dumbstruck, his mouth hanging open, Troy didn't realize what had just happened until Panga nuzzled him with his leathery snout. And then it dawned on him that Panga had just killed the Spinosaur with one deadly blow from his colossal, thrashing tail, breaking the monster's neck.

After thanking his giant pet, and hugs and kisses from Bree, Troy ordered the tame Saltasaur into the lake where he would be safe for the remainder of the night.

Then, after gathering up their water and honey gourds, Troy and Bree dragged the unhurt, but feeble Chief Creta across the sand and into the cave.

There, they spent the night, out of harm's way.

Chapter 13

Troy, Bree, and Chief Creta spent the night in the cave without any further incidents. No other Spinosaurs had ventured near the lake or the cave. Nor had Officer Shuno or his henchmen come calling.

Troy woke up to the maniacal laughter of a lake loon. He yawned, stretched, then rubbed his eyes with his fists. His leg was still sore, but felt much better. His appetite was ravenous, but there was nothing to eat, except the honey, and he would save that for Bree and Chief Creta. He reached over and grabbed the water gourd, pulled the cork, and took a long drink.

He corked the gourd and was setting it down when Bree stirred in her sleep. He noticed her head was resting on the dirt floor, so he scraped some moss from the cave wall and slipped it gingerly beneath her head.

As she slept, he gazed at her and smiled. He noted her soft pouted lips, her long silky hair curled around her shoulders, and her thick dark eyelashes resting high on her smooth cheeks. His heart surged with genuine love for her, and he was thankful for the wonderful blessing he had received.

Life isn't all bad, he thought, stroking her hair. There's a lot of good out there, too. Sometimes it takes a while to find it, though.

As the sun climbed above the eastern treetops, Troy stepped quietly out of the cave and onto the lakeshore.

Panga was standing in the middle of the lake, munching on a mouthful of lake weeds, his body completely submerged except for his head and two feet of his neck.

Troy scanned the shoreline—ignoring the hulking Spinosaur carcass—spotted a fern plant, and picked some of its branches. Then he called softly to Panga, who lumbered from the lake and onto the shore to receive his morning treat.

As Panga chewed, Troy examined his chest wound inflicted last night by the Spinosaur's dagger-like teeth. Thankfully the wound was not serious.

As Troy stared upward, admiring his pet and patting his tree trunk leg, a blast from the town square horn reverberated throughout the surrounding forest.

Time to wake the others, he thought.

It's showtime!

* * *

By the time Troy, Bree, and Chief Creta arrived at the town square, riding on Panga's back, a massive crowd had already gathered there. Among the crowd, standing close to the town square platform, were Troy's mom, Bree's mom, and Mrs. Droma who was holding baby Cera. Little Tyran was at her side, clinging to her leather frock.

Bree's dad was standing on the platform, along with Dr. Hadro, Mr. Droma, and a dozen other men. They were shouting and arguing with Officer Shuno and a handful of his henchmen. Apparently they were so entrenched in their argument, none of them seemed to notice Panga and his three riders who were standing at the end of the path, partially hidden by forest brush. And with hundreds of peoples' backs to them, the crowd didn't notice them, either.

"Then why can't we see him?" Dr. Hadro shouted. "If you didn't kidnap Chief Creta, then let him come downstairs and tell us himself!"

The crowd stirred and murmured.

Officer Shuno thrust his face into Dr. Hadro's, his eyes glaring. "You fool!" he snapped in a hushed voice. "I'll have your head for this!" Then he turned to the crowd and raised his hands, gesturing them into silence. "My fellow villagers, I assure you the Chief has not been kidnapped. My guards have informed me that Dr. Hadro has taken up drinking recently, and for that he must be punished."

The crowd mumbled and appeared agitated.

"As for Chief Creta, I've already told you he has taken very ill and cannot be distur—"

Officer Shuno was interrupted by the sight of Troy steering Panga out of the shadows and into full view of everyone.

As long as Troy lived, he would never forget the utterly shocked look on Officer Shuno's face when Panga plodded forward, the crowd gasping and scrambling to make way for the colossal dinosaur and his three passengers.

Several men from the crowd helped Chief Creta down and walked him up the platform steps, protectively surrounding him.

Troy and Bree slid down on Panga's tail, then ran to their mothers and embraced them.

The crowd bubbled with excitement, chattering incessantly, gesturing with their hands, their faces animated.

Chief Creta—still flanked by his self-appointed bodyguards—hobbled up to Officer Shuno.

Gaping, the crowd immediately fell silent.

Chief Creta cleared his throat, a slight trembling in his feeble body. "Officer Shuno," he began, "you are an utter disgrace to all the people on this island. You betrayed not only me, but more importantly, you have betrayed every man, woman, and child on this island."

The crowd stirred and murmured, then hushed.

"Not only are you not fit to be the Second Commanding Officer," Chief Creta went on, "you are not even fit to live among us. Therefore, I hereby command you and your murderous thugs to a lifetime of imprisonment!"

Things happened quickly then. While the crowd burst alive, ranting and cheering, Officer Shuno and his henchmen were instantly overtaken and bound by several men from the crowd. Chief Creta's bodyguards whisked him out of harm's way, secluding him in a corner.

When the ruckus had died down, and Officer Shuno and his thugs had been safely tied up with their hands behind their backs, Chief Creta hobbled back to center stage and addressed the crowd.

He informed everyone of Officer Shuno's evil plan to take over the island and all its people. He let them know that it was Troy who had saved him, and it was Troy who had kept their best interests at heart, trying to help them with his ideas concerning the boulder, the flower box saltberries, and the saving of baby Cera.

The crowd cheered and applauded. Finally, they hushed, and one man among them hollered, "What do we do now, Chief?"

"Well," said Chief Creta, "I think I'll let Troy answer that one. He's got a lot more good ideas in store for us, and I think we should listen to him." The Chief paused while scanning the crowd. "Troy, will you come up here, please?"

Surprised, Troy pecked his mom and Bree, then made his way through the crowd toward the platform.

The crowd started to applaud and, at the foot of the

platform steps, Mante came up to him, smiling. With him was a beautiful girl who looked to be about the same age. "Way to go, buddy!" Mante said, shaking Troy's hand. He nodded toward the girl. "This is my new girlfriend Permi. Permi, meet my best friend Troy."

"Nice to meet you," said Permi, smiling.

"Same here," Troy called, going up the steps. Smiling, he called to Mante, "Way to go—to you, too!"

The crowd continued applauding until Troy stood on the platform, facing them.

Finally, they were silent.

Troy cleared his throat. "Thank you, everyone. We have a lot of work ahead of us, so I'll make this very brief. But first, I want to say how sorry I am for all of you who lost loved ones last night at the saltberry field. I know firsthand the pain you are suffering from right now. But if my plan works, we'll never have to put peoples' lives in jeopardy, defending our saltberry crop from the Spinosaurs, ever again."

The crowd murmured approval.

"So the first thing we need to do," Troy went on, "is respectfully give our dead a moment of silence before we bury them today."

Numerous people in the crowd bowed their heads, and after a moment of silence, Troy continued.

"We need to divide up into several groups. One group will remove and bury our dead. Another group will plant an entire crop of saltberries at the field. Another group will immediately repair the fence—whatever's left of it after the fire. Another group will search for and gather up as many castor-oil plants as they can find."

The crowd buzzed with curiosity.

Troy explained. "I've discovered—by accident—that castor-oil plants are very poisonous when eaten. So we're going to crush the plants and mix the juice with honey, in order to make a syrup—a very poisonous syrup."

"What'll we do with it?" a man from the crowd yelled.

"We paint it on our fence," said Troy. "Hopefully, if my plan works, the Spinosaurs will be repelled or killed whenever they chew on the fence."

The crowd erupted into cheers and applause.

Enjoying the moment, Troy glanced all around him and noticed Officer Shuno huddled with his henchmen, their hands bound behind them, and Officer Shuno's scowling face red with rage.

The crowd hushed.

"Finally, we need another group to take these buzzards to prison," Troy said, nodding toward Officer Shuno and his henchmen, "and to overpower Steg and the others who are still there, and throw them in prison, too."

He paused, then said, "This is our island, our home, and we can do this, if we all work together. So let's get it done!"

The crowd exploded into cheers and applause.

Chief Creta and Dr. Hadro approached Troy and took turns shaking his hand and patting his back. "Well done, lad," said Chief Creta. "Well done!"

"You really did this island proud, son," said Dr. Hadro.

Troy could barely contain his pride. "Thank you, both," he said, beaming.

Mr. Droma approached, hanging his head, his face sober. He glanced up at Troy, then quickly looked down. "Troy, I don't know what to say. I'm so ashamed. I should've stood behind you, supported you. Especially after you saved my little Cera." He looked up, his eyes misty. "But instead, I betrayed you. And I just wanted to let you know how deeply sorry I am."

He paused. "Can you ever forgive me?"

Looking Mr. Droma in the eye, Troy stuck his hand out and Mr. Droma shook it, surprised and obviously relieved.

"Of course I forgive you," said Troy. "You were only doing what you thought was right at the time."

"Thanks, Troy. I appreciate that." Mr. Droma started to leave, then stopped. "What can I do to help?"

Troy smiled. "Well, I need someone to lead a group of two dozen armed men to take Shuno and his thugs to prison, and throw Steg and the other guards behind bars. And the sooner, the better."

"Consider it done," said Mr. Droma.

Epilogue

Under the cool shade of the storage tree, Troy stood with his hands on his hips, staring at the vast saltberry field. The section of the fence that had burned, had long since been rebuilt, double-thick to match the rest of the fence. The outer fence had been painted with Troy's new invention of castor-oil juice mixed with honey. The resulting product, which he called spinocide, was a raving success. Not a single attack had occurred on the fence since it had been painted with the poisonous syrup.

Troy watched with pride as hundreds of workers labored in harmony, planting an entire field of life-sustaining saltberries, knowing that their crop would never again be ravaged by Spinosaurs.

Hearing voices behind him, he turned and saw Bree and Chief Creta approach him. Bree was carrying a leather sack. Chief Creta walked beside her, holding his cane with one hand and affectionately holding Bree's elbow with the other.

"Hello!" Troy said cheerily.

They greeted him with equal warmth.

"Brought you lunch," said Bree, holding up the sack. "And my parents want you to join us for supper tomorrow."

Troy smiled. "Thanks, Bree. And please tell your folks I'll be there."

Then he turned his attention to Chief Creta. "How are you feeling, Sir?"

"Fine, lad. Just fine, thank you. After a couple of weeks of rest, and plenty of food and water, I feel like a new man."

"I'm glad," Troy said sincerely.

Staring out at the field, the Chief looked pleased. "You've done a good thing here, lad. Your spinocide invention really did the trick." Resting both hands on his cane as he gazed at the workers planting their crop, he sighed. "They're such good people, hard workers. Too bad they have to live their entire lives in fear of Spinosaurs. If only we could eliminate the monsters from this island once and for all."

"Actually," said Troy, "I've been working on a new formula for my spinocide. I've got a lot of experimenting left to do yet, but I think there may be a way to control them. Maybe even exterminate them one day."

"Exterminate the Spinosaurs!" Bree cried.

"Now that really would be something!" Chief Creta said. He looked at Bree and said, "Is there any wonder why I chose *him* to be my Second Commanding Officer?"

She wrapped her arms around Troy. "I'm so proud of you, *Officer* Troy."

Smiling at Troy, the Chief gave Troy a sly wink, his eyes twinkling beneath the bushy brow.

The End

www.ingramcontent.com/pod-product-compliance
Lightning Source LLC
Chambersburg PA
CBHW020617120726
47905CB00003B/836